DopeSick

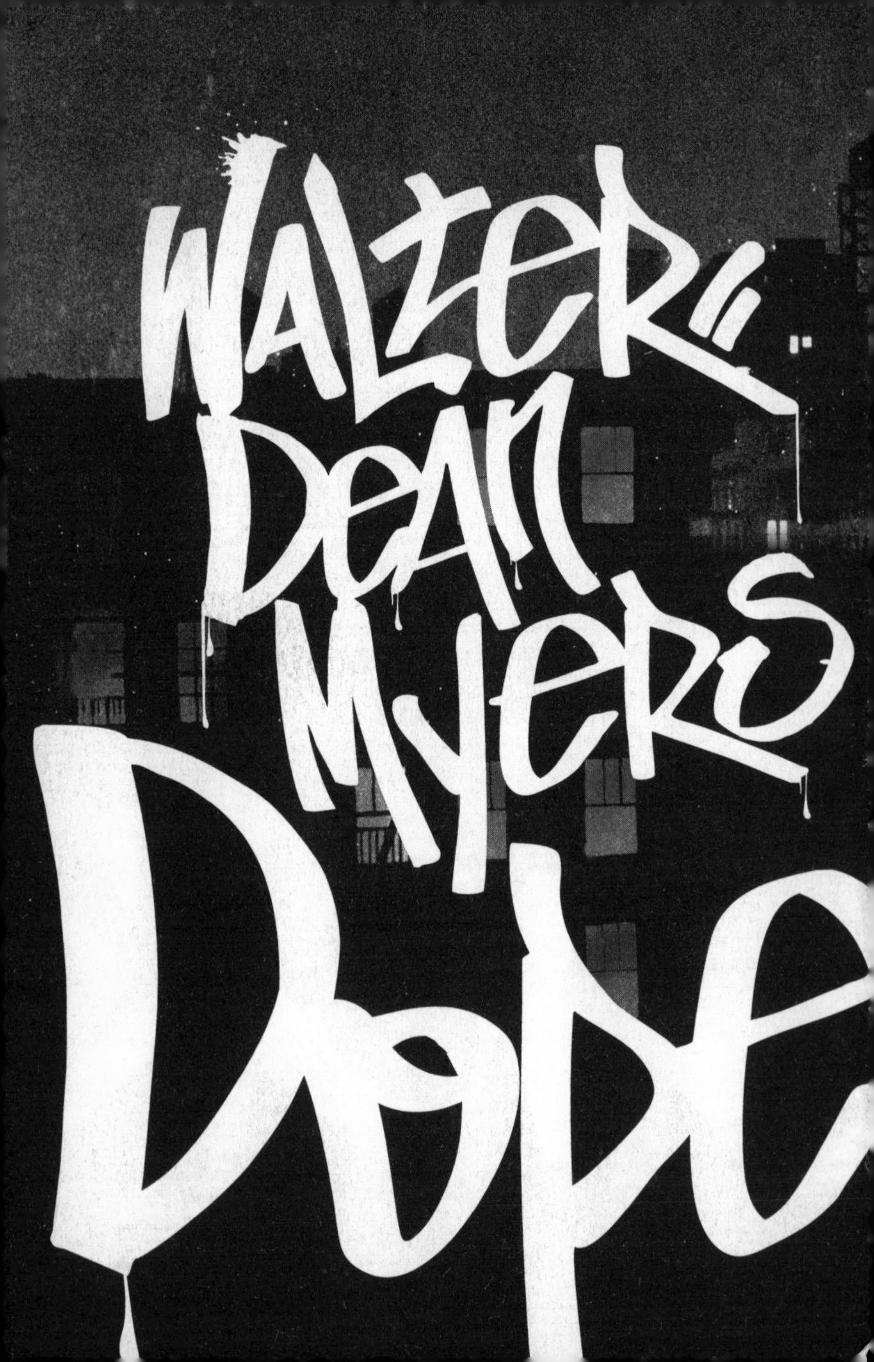
Walter
Dean
Myers
Dope

Sick

Amistad HARPER TEEN
An Imprint of HarperCollinsPublishers

Amistad and HarperTeen are imprints
of HarperCollins Publishers.

Dope Sick

Library of Congress Cataloging-in-Publication Data
Myers, Walter Dean, date
Dope sick / Walter Dean Myers. — 1st ed.
p. cm.
Summary: Seeing no way out of his difficult life in Harlem, seventeen-year-old Jeremy "Lil J" Dance flees into a house after a drug deal goes awry and meets a strange man who shows him different turning points in his life where he could have made better choices.
ISBN 978-0-06-121477-6 (trade bdg.)
ISBN 978-0-06-121478-3 (lib. bdg.)
[1. Conduct of life—Fiction. 2. Drug abuse—Fiction. 3. African Americans—Fiction. 4. Supernatural—Fiction. 5. Harlem (New York, N.Y.)—Fiction.] I. Title.
PZ7.M992Dop 2009 2008010568
[Fic]—dc22 CIP
AC

Typography by Jennifer Heuer
1 2 3 4 5 6 7 8 9 10
❖

First Edition

DopeSick

MY ARM WAS HURTING BAD. Real bad. The bone could have been broken. I couldn't tell. I just knew it was hurting and swollen. I felt like just taking the gun out and throwing it away and giving up so I could get the mess over with. I opened my mouth so I wouldn't make so much noise when I breathed. Down the street I saw the patrol car was still at the corner. He had his lights flashing. I didn't know if he'd seen which way I was running or not. I knew I was too tired to keep running much more.

I started to lift my arm to look at my watch and

the whole arm just lit up with pain. The bone had to be broken. I figured it was two or three o'clock in the morning. Skeeter had called me just past midnight and told me they got Rico. I knew Rico was going to punk out. In a way I was glad they got him, but I knew he was going to blame everything on me.

I was in the shadows in a shop doorway and I knew I couldn't stay there much longer. I had to lie down or sit down or something. Had to get my head together. There was an old building across the street, and it looked like the front door was open. Maybe some juiceheads was in there. I didn't know, but I couldn't stay on the street much more. My arm was hurting too bad, and if that cop had really seen it was me, there would be more cops coming soon.

I felt like crying, like just running down the street and letting them shoot me—anything and everything at the same time. I was messed up big-time and I knew it.

I saw two women walk over to the police car.

Probably hookers out doing their stroll. The cop in the car was talking to them and then he got out and went around the back of the car. I looked to see if he had his gun in his hand. From where I was in the doorway I couldn't see too clear. He might have. I could feel my heart beating fast and my right hand was shaking in my pocket. The cop and the two women walked a little way down the street, and he was up on his toes, trying to look into one of the building windows. I took a deep breath and moved from the doorway to behind a parked car. The street wasn't big and half the buildings didn't have nobody living in them, so it was dark except for the streetlight, and that wasn't working right. Nothing wasn't working right in my life.

I got across the street and into the doorway of the building I had been scoping. Looking down the street, I saw the cop and the two women were still together. The sound of another siren scared me. I couldn't tell where it was coming from. Keeping my eyes on the cop down the street, I pushed on the door behind me with my foot. It opened and I eased into the house.

The smell was terrible. Like somebody had been using it as a piss hole. It was dark except for the light from the cracked-open door. I saw some steps and started thinking about the roof. If I got to the roof, I could come down in another building, maybe even on another block. My left arm was pretty stiff and I didn't want to move it too much. I let go of the Nine I had been carrying since I left my house and fished around in my pockets for some matches. When I found some, I was scared to light them. Maybe the cop had seen me come into the building. Maybe he was just waiting outside for some backup before he came busting in the door.

I put the matches in the pocket with the Nine and started up the steps, walking close to the wall so they wouldn't creak too much.

The smell wasn't no better, but it changed a little as I got near the second floor. It was just that musty smell that old buildings have sometimes. I smelled some vinegar too, so I thought there might have been some dopeheads shooting up in one of the rooms.

I stopped and lit a match, holding the book in my left hand and striking the match with my right. There was garbage on the floor and some piles of old plaster. I seen where the next steps was and started for them. I was being quiet because I didn't want to run into no dopehead or crazy homeless dude.

When I got to the third floor, I heard a sound. It was people talking. I held my breath, trying to figure out if it was somebody who had come in after me or somebody already in the building. My heart was pumping big-time, a mile a minute, and I was feeling sick to my stomach as I leaned against the wall.

Maybe there was a way to figure out where the sound was coming from, but I didn't have that way in me. I was too scared to think good. I knew that if the sound was in the building, it wasn't no cops, so I started up the stairs again. Halfway up the next flight I saw a light coming from under one of the doors. Then I heard the sound again and knew somebody had a television on.

If it was a homeless guy, it would be okay, unless he was crazy and had a knife or an axe or something. If I had to shoot him, the cops might hear it. If it was a doper it would be better. A doper might just be on a nod and might not even wake up.

When I got to the landing, I saw the open door and heard the sound from the television. Somebody talking about how to get some CDs for only $9.99. I slipped past the door and up the last flight to the roof door. I lit another match and saw crack vials and empty Baggies on the landing. I tried to turn the knob on the door leading to the roof, but it didn't move. I got long legs, so I put my back against the door and my foot against the post and pushed hard. Nothing. It didn't move.

For a moment I went crazy inside. I was in the building and couldn't get out to the roof. If anything went down, I knew I'd be trapped.

Calm down, man. Calm down. I tried to talk myself down. *Breathe slow. Breathe slow and get yourself together.* My mouth was dry, but I could feel the cold sweat dripping down my side. My arm hurt real bad. What was the use of keeping on running? If I got infected and had to go to the hospital, they would have me. The bullet was still in my arm and they would just call the police. I imagined being handcuffed to a hospital bed and the cops bringing Rico in to identify me.

Yeah, that's him, I imagined Rico saying. *That's Lil J. He the one who shot the police officer.*

My eyes were closed and I opened them. Had to get out my head and get into the now. Had to think. Maybe there was a fire escape. If I could hit a fire escape, I could still make the roof.

I went down the stairs quick, but still near the banister so I wouldn't make too much noise. If there was a doper in the apartment, he would know how to get out in a hurry. My hands were sweaty and I wiped them off on my pants leg. Had to look cool. Had to look confident.

I took a deep breath outside the door, then pushed it open quick.

It was a long room with a small television on a

table in the corner. There was a dim light on the wall with one of those little yellow lampshades. About six feet in front of the television there was a chair and I could see the back of a dude's head. He could have been on a nod, or just sleeping. He wasn't moving.

I looked around to see what he was about.

"Stay where you are!"

I stopped, realized the Nine was still in my jacket pocket, and took it out. I couldn't see any mirrors so I didn't know if he was seeing me or not. I knew I didn't want to have to shoot this sucker and get the cops pouring into the place, and with my left arm messed up I knew I just couldn't take him out if he had any heart.

"Who you, man?" I asked.

"Kelly," he said.

"Yo, I'm sorry I busted in on you," I said. "Some dudes said I did them wrong and they was chasing me. How I get to the roof?"

The guy didn't turn or nothing, just kept watching the television. I couldn't see his face, but his voice was young. He could have been just a little older than me, maybe eighteen or nineteen.

"There's a chair over there," he said. "Why don't you put your piece away and sit down."

"Man, I ain't got all day," I said, trying to get some bone in my voice. "The fire escape go to the roof?"

"You want to see yourself on television?"

I looked at the windows. There were shades over them and I figured maybe nobody could see the light from outside. I went over and looked out. There was a fire escape. I put my Nine back in my jacket and tried to lift the window.

"It's nailed shut," the guy said. "People don't be leaving their windows open in this neighborhood. You don't know that?"

"Yo, man, what you say your name was?"

"Kelly."

"Well, look, Kelly or Smelly or whatever your name is—I ain't nobody to be playing with," I said. "I'm the one with the Nine pointing at your head."

"Yeah, and you the one stuck in this building

looking for a way out, ain't you?"

Kelly talked street, but I wasn't sure. Something about him wasn't from the 'hood. I wanted to go over to him and put the Nine against his neck, but for some reason I didn't think it was going to bother him. The sucker might have been crazy.

"You know a way out?" I asked.

"Why don't you cop a squat and check yourself out on the tube," Kelly said. He was looking at the television.

I looked at the television and saw the street below. It looked empty.

"You got the television hooked up to security cameras?" I asked.

"No."

"Then how come . . . ?" On the television there was a person moving across the street, wearing a dark jacket. He had one hand up by his side and the other in his jacket pocket. It was me.

"What is this, a movie or something?"

"Yeah. I guess it's a movie. What part you want to see next?"

"You ain't got nothing better to do with your ass than take pictures of people in the street and watch them?" I asked.

"What's your name?" Kelly asked.

"Roger," I said. "Roger Jones."

"Yeah, then why they calling you 'Lil J' on television?"

"That was on the news?"

"They said you popped a cap in a cop."

"They said he died?"

Kelly pointed the remote toward the screen and clicked it twice. A white guy with blond hair came on.

> *In the news today: Yet another officer shot in the line of duty. Thirty-three-year-old Anthony Gaffione was shot on Harlem's east side during an undercover drug bust in what police officials identify as "drug alley." Gaffione, a seven-year veteran, is reported in critical condition at Columbia Presbyterian Hospital,*

where he spent three hours in surgery this afternoon. One suspect, nineteen-year-old Rico Brown, was captured in the Bronx. The shooter, identified as seventeen-year-old Jeremy Dance, known as 'Lil J,' is still being sought.

In Basra, Iraq, yesterday . . .

Kelly clicked the remote and the television was showing the street again.

"I didn't do the shooting," I said.

"What happened?" Kelly asked.

"What difference do it make?" I said. "If he dies and they get me, I am never getting out of jail. If he doesn't die and they get me, I still am never getting out of jail. My life is just flushed, man."

"If you could do it all over again, and change something, what would it be?" Kelly asked.

"Shut up with that bullshit!" I said.

He shut up and neither of us spoke for a while. On the television the picture of me standing in the doorway, looking down the street, played over and over again. I didn't know how Kelly had taken it, but it was depressing to see. I looked scared and I was holding my left arm folded up high by my side. I hadn't realized I was doing that. You could see it was hurt and something was wrong with the way I was looking around. Maybe that was why the cop in the patrol car had pulled me over. Maybe he hadn't recognized me.

I went over and looked out the window. There was nothing right down front, but there were at least two police cars near the corner and some more flashing lights from other cars parked around the corner reflected off the windows of the buildings across the street. It was October and getting kind of cold, and the cops had their hands in their pockets. I pulled down the shade. Every cop in New York was going to be looking for me. They would have their guns out too.

"Hey, Kelly, you live here?" I asked.

"Sometimes."

"Look, you seem like you okay," I said. "I didn't shoot that cop. Rico shot him. Square business.

You know a way out of this building?"

"Ain't no use running," Kelly came back. "Where you going to go?"

"I'll take my chances if I can get to the roof," I said. "See what happens from there."

"You want to see what happens?" Kelly reached for the remote again. He pointed it at the television, and now the picture showed the street again, but this time the street was full of police cars.

I ran to the window and looked down. Nothing.

"It's on fast forward," Kelly said. "It's what's going to happen."

"Yo, what kind of spooky crap is this?"

"You want to see what's going to happen?" Kelly asked. "It don't make me no never mind. You don't want to see, it's okay."

I didn't say nothing, just nodded toward the television. The chair that Kelly had told me to sit in was wood, and one of the legs was a little wobbly. I rubbed my left arm as the image of the street below, full of cops and police cars, played over the set.

Some of the police had on SWAT suits, complete

with helmets and rifles. Then I came on the screen. Somehow I had made it to the roof. I saw me looking over the side. Then there was an image of a SWAT team coming up the stairs. Then there was me again. I was sitting against the low brick wall at the edge of the roof. Then the SWAT team had reached the roof landing. And then I was lifting the Nine, but my eyes were closed, there were tears running down my face, and I was holding the Nine against my own head.

"Stop it!"

Kelly clicked it off quick. "You okay, man?" he asked.

"No." I was shaking.

"So if you could take back one thing you did," Kelly asked, "what would it be?"

"Take back the day that cop was shot," I said. "Just that one day."

Kelly turned and shot a quick glance in my direction. Then he clicked the remote again.

THE DUDE CLICKED THE REMOTE, and all of a sudden I was seeing myself on the screen. It was like I was in my own head again, looking out of my own eyes at the world. It was weird, but like I couldn't turn away because it was me all over again, me outside of me digging on what was going on in my head. I seen the door to my room at home and my moms looking in and talking to me.

"Lil J, you 'wake?"

"Yeah."

"Can you go down to the clinic for me?"

"What time is it?"

"When it opens."

"What time is it?

"I don't know."

I turned and looked at the small red alarm clock on the dresser. Seven o'clock. I swung my legs over the side of the pull-out bed and sat up. I put my elbows on my knees and rested my head in my hands.

"Lil J, can you go for me?" Mama's voice was flat, raspy.

"Yeah, Ma." My mouth felt as if it was lined with dirty cotton. It was Wednesday, and I was supposed to go downtown with Maurice to look for a job.

I heard water running in the kitchen and hoped Mama had put on her housecoat. She was getting careless about things like that and I didn't like it. It was worrisome. What I wanted to do was to get some money together and send her down to Grandma Lois in Curry, North Carolina. The last time she had been down there, she came back looking good and feeling good for the first time.

Grandma Lois didn't allow any drinking, and Curry was such a two-stick town, you couldn't get anything else.

I got up and went out to the bathroom. Mama had her housecoat on. She had already put the water on and was shaking coffee from the can into the percolator. She looked at me as I went through the kitchen.

"What you doing today?" she asked.

"Maurice heard about jobs coming up at Home Depot," I said. "We going down there and check it out."

Mama grunted in reply.

I sat on the toilet. I liked to see my black thighs against the white porcelain. It was the one thing that Mama did that was cool, was to keep the bathroom clean. Other than that she was always too sick, or too drunk, to take care of any kind of business. When I was small and we were living on 147th Street, she used to tell me how her main chore as a kid was keeping the bathroom clean.

"Your grandma Lois used to say, 'Girl, that

bathroom so clean, I need to ask your permission to use it! '"

Grandma Lois had her thing together. It was a church kind of thing, but she had a lot of pride, and it hurt her to see Mom, her only daughter, get knocked around. When Grandma Lois had the chance to go down to Curry, she thought hard and long about leaving Arlena, but in the end she knew she wasn't doing her any good in Harlem, so she left, hoping to build up something down in North Carolina that would make Mom want to join her.

I washed up and thought about what I would tell the people down at Home Depot. First thing I would have to do is lie about my age. I would say I was nineteen so they wouldn't ask me nothing about why I wasn't in school. I had my fake GED in a plastic sleeve along with my Social Security card. I thought about saying that I'd taken some time off after high school because I was thinking about joining the army, but then I thought that probably wouldn't work.

Home Depot was the joint. I knew if I could

cop a job with them, I could get my thing together. Maybe I would find another place for me and Mama or even convince her to go down to North Carolina. I knew she didn't want to go down with nothing in her pockets.

"I don't want nobody feeling sorry for me," she said. "They can think what they want, but I don't want to be explaining nothing to nobody."

I could dig that. If you had some money in your pocket, you could walk on your own side of the street and let people walk on they side. If it went down correct, I could send her some money every week and then she wouldn't have to ask for nothing. That's what life was about, being able to take care of your own business.

"The clinic opens at eight thirty," Mama said. She was sitting at the table, making a circle with her fingers around the flowered coffee cup. She had nice fingers, long and slender. If she had had her nails done, they would've looked good.

"You got pains in your stomach again?"

"It's just nervous," she said. "You look like you

going to a funeral in that white shirt. Is that new?"

"Yeah," I answered. "Told you I got a job interview."

"Well, you should get it, as fine as you looking today," Mama said. She had a smear of something white on her cheek.

"You coughing again?"

"You a doctor now?" she answered, smiling.

"Doctor Dance," I answered. "Yo, that's hip."

The coffee she made was way too weak. I needed something strong in the morning.

"Where your prescription?" I asked.

"It's on the refrigerator, in the bowl," she said. "When you coming home?"

"Depends on how long the interview takes," I said. "They ain't in a hurry, 'cause they got their job already."

Mama said she really needed the medicine because she had run out, and I said I would be home as soon as I could.

The prescription was for painkillers. I went into the bathroom and looked through Mama's little lineup of plastic containers. I thought I had seen some of the pills she was looking for and found them. I opened the childproof container and dumped the pile out in my hand. There were eight pills left. I put four in my pocket and took the others out to Mama.

"Where were these?" she asked.

"On the second shelf," I said.

I watched her take two pills with coffee and put two back in the container for later.

I was supposed to meet Maurice on 125th Street and St. Nicholas. We were thinking on going over to the Home Depot interview together. I wanted both of us to get jobs, but I still hoped that Maurice didn't look too much better than me.

I was glad I had spent the money for a new shirt even though it had left me with less than three dollars.

Maurice was five nine, two inches shorter than me, but broad. We had talked about going into the army together and maybe going to Iraq.

"You don't hear nothing much about guys going

to Iraq unless they get killed," Maurice said. "You ever notice that? You hear about guys being on trial or guys being blown up, but you don't hear anything about guys fighting their way out of a trap or taking a hill or anything like that."

"It ain't that kind of war," I had said.

In the end we had both decided not to join up. I didn't mention nothing about how maybe the army wouldn't take me because of what had happened down in Texas. I didn't want Maurice to know about that.

We had checked each other out and said we was looking good, and then we had walked over to where they were having the interviews.

"Man, please don't tell me that's the line for the job interviews," Maurice said, looking down the block. "Just don't tell me that."

It was the line. It stretched a full half block down from the store, and more people were coming every moment.

"How many jobs they got?" I asked.

"They said in the paper they had six openings,"

Maurice said. "My mother said they probably had about ten or twelve, but this is stupid. Look, that dude even got his dog with him."

I felt sick. I had really been hoping for the job. I looked over the line and knew it wasn't going to happen. There were young men, old men, women, Spanish, whites—everybody was out looking for some kind of work.

"I can't cut this," I said to Maurice. "I'll come back later."

"I'm gonna hang." Maurice shrugged. "I don't have nothing better to do."

I told Maurice I was going to get Mama's prescription filled and would be back later to see how the line looked. I remembered that Rico had called me last night and asked me if I wanted to run some work. I had said no, putting all my hopes on the Home Depot gig, but that looked like a bust. I hoped I had some minutes on my cell, and called Rico.

"Yo, man, that thing still going?" I asked when Rico answered.

"Yeah, it's still on," Rico said. "Where you at?"

"A Hundred and Twenty-fifth and St. Nicholas, outside the church."

"Okay, I'll be there in ten minutes. Hang loose."

I knew that Rico was a stone viper, but sometimes he came up with some crazy money. He was steady dealing weed, Girl, or anything else he could get his hands on. He also had a hundred-dollar-a-day jones he had to support.

I went down the street to a little candy store and bought a bottle of soda. I took two of the pain killers I had brought along and tried to think what Rico sounded like on the phone. If Rico was right, far enough away from his first hit of the day to have his head straight but not pushing so close to the next hit that he would be dope sick, everything would be cool. I had seen Rico dope sick a bunch of times, licking his lips, acting all jumpy, his eyes darting around as if he was a wolf looking for some sick animal to jump on.

Rico wasn't somebody you could rely on and he had messed me up before. But just the way Rico got dope sick, the way he turned into something that wasn't good to see, I was getting broke sick. I was tired of walking the streets with nothing in my pockets, and nothing coming down the way. When Mama got her check, she gave me what she could and sometimes I got some pickup work, but that hardly paid enough to eat on. I could work a full day and come home with less than forty dollars. If I couldn't find no pickup job and Mama didn't have no money, then there wasn't anything to do except stand on the corner wishing I was somewhere else or home staring at the stupid crap on television.

Rico's ten minutes stretched into a half hour. I was about to call him again when I saw him coming up out the subway.

"Yo, man, what's happening?" Me and Rico bumped fists.

"Nothing, man," I said. "What you got?"

"I got a run for Dusty Phillips," Rico said. "Three loads. That's a hundred for each load."

"Where we got to take it?"

"Across from Marcus Garvey Park," Rico said. "No problem."

Yeah. No problem. I knew there was always a problem. Dusty wouldn't be sending out runners and spreading his money if there wasn't any room for some fuckery. We went up the street to Dusty's place and I started talking about the Yankees. Rico was always tripping, and I needed to see how far gone he was already. He seemed sharp enough, so I started to chill a little.

If everything went down right and I copped a full Benjamin and a half, I would split over to the Home Depot line. I'm good with some cash in my pocket, so I could go into the interview feeling righteous and looking confident. I could look the Man in the eye and say I wanted the job and could handle anything. And that was the truth when my life was on the money. I wouldn't be just another broke-sick fool begging for a slave.

I let my mind go free, even as I was talking to Rico about the Yankees. Rico was getting on the Yankee infielders for not hitting more home runs.

"If you making big bucks, you need to be getting big hits," Rico was saying.

Yeah, all that was good. But I didn't dream about making big money. I just dreamed about getting a decent crib for me and Mama, a steady job, and, most of all, not being broke sick.

Dusty Phillips had some hard-ass people working for him, some ugly mothers who look like they went to their first communion in them orange jumpsuits prisoners be wearing. He operated from the back of a ninety-nine-cent store. They hardly had anything in the store, and everybody in the neighborhood knew not to go in there. Once in a while they got a legitimate customer and were nasty enough and scary enough to discourage him from coming back.

Dusty used to be called Blinky when he was a kid growing up on 116th Street because he had a nervous twitch and his eyes looked a little off. It was like he was trying to look at you, but his eyes kept moving away from where you were. When he got older and fought his way big-time into the game, he told people to call him Dusty, and after he shot a guy who called him Blinky, everybody else got the picture.

We got to his joint and Dusty looked me over like I was something that stunk bad. He asked Rico if I was all right, and Rico said I was.

"Y'all meet this white boy at two o'clock. Give him the dope and make damn sure the money you get from him is correct. Then you get that money to me by three this afternoon." Dusty's voice was high and he talked fast. "If my money don't come back correct, everybody is going to be sorry. Anything I'm saying is confusing you?"

"No, man," Rico said. "I'm hip."

We got the dope from Dusty, all wrapped up in a plastic sandwich Baggie, and took it to Rico's pad on 135th Street across from the House of Prayer for All People. As soon as we were inside and had locked the doors, Rico took out the bags of heroin and counted the glassine envelopes in each one. Then he opened a bag, sniffed it, and passed it to me.

"We can tap this nice," Rico said.

"You don't be tapping Dusty's stuff," I said. "You ain't stupid. If the white boy don't buy it, what we going to do, take it back to Dusty all tapped out?"

"Yeah, you're right," Rico said. "But we can tap a buzz, right?"

I thought that Dusty knew that Rico would tap the loads, taking just a little bit from each bag for himself. But if the dope was as good as everybody said Dusty's stuff was, it would probably be all right. What I didn't want was Rico getting high and blowing the whole deal. And what I definitely didn't want was to mess up completely and get Dusty on our case.

I watched while Rico tapped a few bags from each load, enough to make a half bag for himself. We had an hour to go before the drop, and I figured that a half bag wouldn't mess with Rico's head too much, seeing that it was a long way from his regular eight-to-ten-bag jones.

"You need a hit?" Rico asked as he cooked up the dope.

"Nah," I said. "I'm good."

What I didn't say was that I wasn't into no dealing. The Man catch you with a taste and you get a slap on the wrist. You get caught with enough to deal and you catching calendars. I'd rather die than face fifteen to twenty years in jail.

Still, I copped a bag when Rico started his nod, figuring I could bring it up if I needed to.

I'M SITTING THERE WATCHING the whole thing on television, watching my life like it was happening outside my body. The whole thing was fascinating and scary at the same time. I could even feel my body moving when I saw myself on the screen. It was like I was in two places at the same time, being two people, with one of them looking inside the other, checking out his own mind.

"Then what happened?" Kelly had a way of kind of hunching his shoulders when he talked, like he was pushing the words up.

"You think people in the street can see the

lights from the television?" I asked.

Kelly clicked the remote and we were looking at the street again. There were three police cars, and some of the officers were looking up at a building, but it wasn't the one we were in.

"Then what happened?" Kelly asked again.

"We waited around for a while and Rico tapped the lid again. He got another half bag, cooked that up, and hit the line. That kind of freaked me out, because I figured he might just go on tapping and cooking up the stuff until he blew the whole gig."

"Then he wouldn't be able to go with the sale?"

"Yeah. So I called him on it," I said. "If the deal didn't go down, we could say the white boy didn't show correct or we saw some wrong-looking dudes hanging around. But if the dope was light when we took it back to Dusty, we were going to have to take the heat, you know what I mean?"

"Yeah. You scared of Dusty."

"So then it was time to go do the thing and Rico had said we should carry a piece in case somebody tried to rip us off," I said. "I didn't think no white boy trying to cop in the middle of Harlem was looking to rip nobody off, so it wasn't a big thing. Rico was feeling nice, but he wasn't really high yet, so it looked like a bet."

"You wasn't using nothing?" Kelly asked.

"No, I ain't stupid, man. I just needed to get paid. Drugs and business don't go together."

"I always wondered why they put those candles on the sidewalk," Kelly said.

"What candles?"

"You know, where they find the body," he came back. "They put candles on the street and write stuff on the wall like 'June Bug, we love you,' and 'RIP.' "

"That's a memorial to whoever it was got killed," I said. "You didn't know that? Where you live? If you from around here, you should know that."

"Yeah, I know that, but why candles and flowers after the killing when half the time they didn't even know the dude before he got killed? Or some girl got killed or some baby got killed," Kelly said. "Don't make no sense to me."

"So you ain't the smartest sucker in the world," I said. "Nothing wrong with that. But those candles and the flowers and the good-byes written on the wall is like a sign of respect and love."

"Why you showing love to somebody you don't know?"

"Later for all this mouth running." I was getting tired. "How I'm going to get out of here?"

"You think the police are creeping up on you?"

The truth was that Kelly was creeping up on me. He was making me jumpy. He looked like street and he talked like street, but something was telling me different.

"All I want to do is get some distance from here," I said. "That's straight up. You got some ideas how I can do that?"

"By changing something you did," Kelly said, "making it all different. Look to me like you've been making garbage for a while and dragging it with you. Now you need to get out of here, and that garbage is weighing you down."

Somebody had their radio going, and I heard

it playing a drum-and-bass jam. It was pounding like my heart was pounding, but it had more rhythm.

"I'm going to make something different with that television and your remote?" I asked. "You got to come up with a stronger line than that, man."

"You got a better idea?" Kelly asked. "You standing here shaking and sweating and wondering if you gonna make it through the night. You ain't got nothing going on, so you might as well keep watching the tube and working your brain to figure out where you need to be making some changes."

"Did I tell you that you're a spooky-ass chump?"

"I don't know about the chump part, but I like being spooky," Kelly said. "You know, like you meet up with somebody in the dark and they see you spooky, they start paying attention. Like you paying attention."

"Whatever. Anyway, I'm still working on that day. If that day was different."

"You mean getting up in the morning?" Kelly

asked. "You want to stay in bed?"

"That might have helped, but I'm really talking about what happened with the cop," I said. "Yo, you got any aspirins up in here?"

"Your arm hurting?"

"Why you think I need the aspirins? You know my arm is hurt."

"Okay, so let's get back to yesterday and the cop." Kelly ignored my arm hurting. "Rico was tasting Dusty's stuff, but you wasn't using nothing?"

"How many times I got to tell you?" I said.

"Three's a good number," Kelly said. "But it don't make no never mind to me. You the one looking for a change. I don't need to change."

"You sitting up here by yourself watching television in this stink hole is what you want to be doing?" I asked. "You look like you need a change to me."

"Check it out, Lil J," Kelly said. "You got the Nine and all I got is the remote and the television looking out on the world. But I can walk on out of here and go crosstown and cop a burger and some fries if I want. If I want, I can smile all the way like I'm crazy or ask people for spare change or just stand on the corner and watch the world go by. You can't do none of that without maybe getting gunned down, so why you still up in my face running game?"

"So what you want to know?"

"Like I said before"—Kelly's head turned a little, but I still didn't see his full face—"Rico was tasting Dusty's stuff, but you wasn't using nothing?"

"I don't hit the line, but sometimes I skin-pop," I said. "Just a little under the skin when I'm down. I used to party all the time, but I know . . ."

"You know what you know, right?"

"Yeah."

"You scared of hitting the line?" Kelly asked.

"I heard a lot of bad things happening when dudes be shooting dope right in their veins," I said. "Infections. You get some bad dope and put it right in your vein—you can be dead before you know it. I'm a little scared of needles anyway. I figured I wouldn't get hep C or AIDS or nothing if I just skin-popped."

"You got to work hard to be that ignorant, but if you going to dope it up, you might as well be ignorant, because it's all going the same way," Kelly said.

"You don't know that."

"I know you got to lie about even using," Kelly said.

"I use, but I'm not really into a trick bag," I said. "You know what I mean?"

"So, tell me what happened with the cop."

I sat down on the armrest of a stuffed chair. It smelled a little pissy, but I didn't care. I was really getting tired. "Me and Rico got the stuff together and wrapped it in that plastic Baggie you put food in when it got to go in the freezer," I said. "We put a little tape around it, so in case the white boy got nervous, he wouldn't want to take the time to unwrap it. Maybe he would just want to give up the cash and return to wherever he came from.

"Rico was down from his nod and was grinning and bopping the way he do when he's high. I was mellow, but I was okay. You know, I wasn't nervous or anything. That's the way dope does me. I still got the same things going on in my head, but it's like I don't care that much anymore. We got down where we was supposed to meet the guy with the cash—he was supposed to be wearing a jacket and a green-and-yellow sweater that said FUTBOL. I spot the dude and Rico goes over to him and says something while I hold on to the drugs. Then we go into the building.

"I'm checking the dude out and he's jumpy, like he's anxious to get the stuff. I figure him to be a dude using big-time and needing to get right. I check his hands, and he's got tracks on the back of his left hand—you know, maybe he's right-handed and running out of road—and he's been hitting the veins there too hard. But I was getting nervous, too. I'm sensing the set ain't correct."

"Your high wearing off?" Kelly asked.

"No, the white boy is getting me nervous," I said. "He's all jumpy and everything, but he's chubby, too. You know, if he's that heavy into horse, running up to Harlem to buy it from strangers, how he spending so much money on food he staying chubby?

"I looked the guy right in the eye and said, 'Rico, this fool ain't right.' Meanwhile, Rico got the money and the guy was scoping the dope and trying to pull out a bag from a hole he punched in the plastic with his finger. He looked up at me and then at Rico, and Rico pulled his piece, put it upside the guy's neck, and told him not to move. Rico felt around his waist and didn't feel no piece and said he was all right. But I knew if he was a cop he might have his piece on his ankle and I told Rico to check his ankle. Then everything broke out.

"The cop hit Rico with his shoulder and tried to push him back, but Rico got the gun up again and told the cop to chill or he would blow his ass away. Then the cop said for us to chill and everything would be okay. He was calm too. I went down to his ankle and found his gun.

"Rico said we was taking the dope and the money, which was the right thing to do. Then we asked him if he had some handcuffs, and he did. We handcuffed the fool to the banister. We knew he had some backup outside, but we had another way of getting out the hallway. We told the cop if he hollered we were going to come and shoot him. We started down the hall and Rico, thinking with his dope instead of his head, said he was going to check to see if the cop had a wallet. I told him we needed to get up out of there, but he went back. I heard the guy saying 'Don't shoot me, don't shoot me!' Then . . . *Pop! Pop! Pop!*"

"Rico just wasted the dude?" Kelly asked.

"Yeah. Yeah. Then he run by me toward the door. We come running out through a yard. There was a cop in the yard in plainclothes. He had on a uniform like the ones the guys who climb poles to fix telephone lines wear. We surprised him and Rico took a shot at him. I jumped the fence and started running, and Rico must have jumped after me. I felt something hit my arm. I didn't even know I had been shot. You know, the adrenaline was pumping."

"You were scared."

"Yeah. Yeah. I was so scared, I couldn't even catch my breath. I was like huffing and trying to suck in some air. I ran down the street, cut through an alley, and then wound up back on the street. I was down on 122nd Street, across from where that warehouse used to be. There was nothing happening on the street except a whole crowd of brothers hanging out, as usual. I slowed down to a walk and headed downtown. I wanted to run, but I was trying to keep cool at the same time."

"Why you keep the cop's gun?"

"How you know . . . ? I was scared to have it on me and scared to throw it away. I was in, like, a panic. You know what I mean? I knew if the cop was dead, it was going to be all over if they got us. You can't kill a cop and look for mercy. We could have got away clean if Rico hadn't gone back for the cop's wallet. He probably didn't even have no wallet on him.

"I circled around and went uptown to Harlem

Hospital and got some coffee in that little restaurant right off the lobby. The guy had the news on, but there wasn't nothing about the deal, and for a while I thought maybe the guy wasn't a cop and maybe Rico hadn't really shot him anyway."

"You believed that?"

"Naw, but I wanted to believe it. I really didn't know what to believe. All the time I was thinking about what had happened and steady hoping for the best. At home I told my mother that they had run out of her medicine and I would get it in the morning. She asked me if I had got the job and I said no. I had the Baggie from Dusty's loads, and I cooked that in the bathroom and popped it so I could relax."

"Why you say you weren't using?" Kelly asked.

"It ain't really your business," I said.

"What? What you say?"

"Nothing, man. I know I was using. I ain't happy with it or nothing like that," I said. "You don't be getting off scraping the streets looking for no dope and you don't be getting off being half sick all the time."

"You nodded out?"

"No, I was too uptight. I lay across my bed in the dark feeling bad. Rico called me and said he had taken the money over to Dusty and he had some cash and a taste for me. I wanted to ask him if he had killed the cop, but I guess I didn't want to know. He sounded like nothing had went down, like it was some cowboy movie and we could just move on. Then Skeeter called me, real late, and told me that the cops had picked up Rico. He asked me if I knew what Rico had done. I said no."

"So what you did you want to change?" Kelly asked.

"I want to change going with Rico in the first place," I said.

"Just get you out this mess and you be straight?"

"Not really," I said. "But I won't be facing no cop-shooting charge. They got Rico, and I know he's going to rat me out. Then I got twenty-five years to life if the cop lives. If he don't live I'm going to be facing . . . you know. . . ."

"The rest of your life in jail?"

"Yeah."

"So you want to be back looking at the line at Home Depot and thinking how you so lucky you ain't in jail?" Kelly asked. "What you call it—broke sick? That's where you want to be?"

"I'm not saying that's what I want altogether," I said. "But what I'm saying is, if I could get out this mess, maybe I could do something good with my life."

"Like what?"

"I don't know *like what*!"

"Okay, like how?"

"Look, Kelly, you might be okay, or you might be some kind of nut," I said. "I don't know. I know I'm tired of talking to your ass. I know I'm tired of thinking about what I should have done yesterday. I know I'm just tired. If I knew what to do with my life, how to fix it up, I would have done it a long time ago. You can't dig that? You think I want to live like I'm somebody's throwaway? I want the same thing as you want—no, not like you want, because I don't want to live in no abandoned building watching television and being spooky. You know what I would like to be doing?"

"What?"

"I'd like to be living in a regular house doing something with Lauryn. She's my son's mama."

"You got a son?"

KELLY LIFTED THE REMOTE and my eyes automatically went to the television. The screen was full of bright, jagged lines that slanted one way and then the other. Then the picture cleared and I saw some guys in loose white outfits. They were doing karate or jujitsu or something like that. There was a figure up front—I could only see the side of his head. The camera seemed to turn to him, and at first I didn't know who it was. Then I saw it was my boy Maurice. Just like before, I was seeing the scene and thinking about it in my head at the same time.

"Why you holding your breath?" Kelly asked.

I didn't answer him. I was thinking that every time I told Kelly a lie, he could turn and see the truth on his television. I didn't want to lie to him, but sometimes I couldn't help myself. I watched as the camera zoomed in on Maurice. When he spoke, I knew exactly what he was going to say.

"Why she gotta sound like that?" Maurice asked me. We were at St. John's in Brooklyn watching some tae kwon do guys work out.

"Yo, man, Lauryn's mother is just one of those chicks who come off dead wrong and don't give a damn," I said. "She know she got me in a bind, and she's working it."

"Yeah, but saying you can't even go see your own baby . . ." Maurice shook his head. "Everybody's talking about how guys walk away from their baby mama, and you're stepping up to the plate and she's still talking that ugly talk."

"You don't know the half of it," I said. "Hey, Mo, check out this brother with the dreads."

Me and Maurice had both taken some lessons in tae kwon do. Maurice had lived in Jersey City for a while and took lessons with some Korean guy named Park. I had taken some lessons at Milbank, but I wasn't sweet with it like Maurice.

"They call him Rasta Jesus," Maurice said. "He's supposed to be trying out for the World Games."

"Rasta Jesus? That's a tough name."

Rasta Jesus was smooth and quick and about six seven, maybe even six eight. I wondered why anybody that big would even get into tae kwon do. Me and Maurice were thinking about taking some more lessons, but the guys we saw in the class at St. John's looked way too good. We'd be doing catch-up for three years.

"You want to start back?" Maurice asked.

"Yeah."

We copped the A for the long ride back from Brooklyn, mostly talking about Rasta Jesus and the class we had just seen. I was talking on the tae kwon do, but my mind was on Lauryn and how her mama wouldn't let me come to the apartment.

"This is my apartment and I'm going to say who

comes in and who don't come in and I don't care who likes it and who don't!" she said, shaking her fat finger in front of my face and wiggling her ugly head. "You want to see Brian, then you get your own apartment, and if she want to raise him up there, she can. But she ain't bringing him to your mama's house, because I don't like what's going on, and you know what I mean!"

I felt like punching her in her face, but I knew that wouldn't do any good. Really, I thought she wanted me to hit her. A lot of people do that, try to sucker you into doing a hurry-up so you come off looking stupid. I wasn't going for it, but she had me feeling bad.

Me and Moms was living in Section 8 housing, and I thought that if Lauryn and me got married, we could get our own place. A week after Lauryn had Brian, we had went down to the welfare office and talked to some punk interviewer who ran us through a lot of garbage about the rules of Section 8 and how I had to be working and earning a minimum wage and all that.

"If I had all that hooked up, I wouldn't be down here talking to you," I said.

Lauryn said I shouldn't have lost my temper.

"Why you getting mad all the time?" she asked me outside the dingy-looking building on 14th Street. "He's got to say what he's got to say because that's his job."

"Hey, girl, this is supposed to be a place where you can catch a break, right?" I answered. "You see all them junkies and guys who just got out of jail and stuff? They running up, signing for their checks, and getting into the wind. We trying to make it as a family and we got to hear his mouth."

"Lil J, you need to have an attitude check, baby," Lauryn said. "There's just two things going down. You either walk away when people get into your face or you don't. If you got the cash to walk away, then you don't have to take nothing. But if you ain't got the cash to dash, you got to take their stuff. You know that, so why are you tripping over what he had to say?"

"Don't go white on me, Lauryn," I said.

"Don't do *what*?" Lauryn turned and looked at me. "Don't go *white* on you?"

She sucked her teeth and picked up her stride as we walked toward Sixth Avenue. I caught up with her and tried to take her hand, but she pulled it away.

"Hey, I'm sorry," I said. "I didn't mean nothing."

"If you didn't mean *nothing*, you'd better inform your mouth, because evidently your lips were meaning *something*!" she said.

I took Lauryn home, or at least to the door, and that's when her mama ran the whole thing about how I couldn't come into her house. Normally, Lauryn would have been in my corner, but she was mad and didn't speak up.

What I believed was that Lauryn's mama was trying to bust us up. The first thing she had done was to get Lauryn to name the baby Brian, after Lauryn's father. Brian Alexander had died when Lauryn was four years old, and she hardly remembered him at all. I didn't want the baby named Jeremy, after me, because I don't like "Juniors," but I thought he could have a name starting with a *J*, which would be like saying that he was my kid and everything.

Me and Lauryn had talked about raising a family. She's sweet and she's smart. When I first met her, I didn't think I could even come close to pulling her. In the first place she was fine. She was five six, almost five seven, with a cute face and full lips that looked like somebody should be kissing them all the time. But mostly it was how she carried herself. She didn't come off like no round-the-way girl but more like somebody leaving where they were expected to be and heading for where they needed to get to and was steady on her way. It didn't take me but two times going out with her to know she had my heart. Plus we been through some stuff together. Things were getting heavy for me, and when I slipped from dibbing and dabbing into drugs, from weekend parties to really getting wired up, she helped me do a serious pull-back. What she said was the same old same old about how drugs mess you up. I knew that like everybody else. But I knew she meant it just for me and it was coming from way inside her, and that meant something. I cut back some. I wasn't completely correct, and she knew it, but I wasn't sleeping with King Kong every day either.

Sometimes when things got real bad, when I was dope sick like a mother, she would just hold me and ask me to dream with her.

"What you want to dream about?" I asked.

"Let's dream about you going out to work in the morning and me being home taking care of our two-point-two children—they say that's the average among black people—and then you come home and we can have dinner and talk or maybe watch television," Lauryn said. "Then I'll read a story to the children and put them to bed and then we'll go to bed. You want to know what our bedroom is going to look like?"

"How we going to have two-point-two children?" I asked. "We're either going to have two or three. You can't have a *point-two* child."

"So you want to have three kids?"

"Two's enough," I said.

She would go on about how the bedroom would look, and sometimes she would cut out pictures from magazines showing how somebody had fixed up their living room or playroom. She picked out some nice-looking rooms, too.

All that was so good. The dreaming, the talking way past midnight. It was like she was putting those dreams up against the dope. The dope was making holes in me. I knew that, and Lauryn was plugging them up. She could make me feel like I was somebody. Maurice, my main man, said that when I was with Lauryn, I used to even look like I was in love.

Then she told me she was pregnant. When she was saying it, I was smiling, like I was happy. I *was* happy too, because I thought about all the things we had said, about how I was going to be coming home at night and her reading to the children, and all. But Lauryn was serious as she talked. I could see the worry in her face.

All those dreams we had talked about were like

clouds floating high in the sky, far above Real. It wasn't that we didn't know that—we knew it good. But together we could just look at each other and not look down to where Real was waiting. Being pregnant changed that in a minute. Real jumped up, grabbed me, and started shaking hard. It was like Real was saying, *Let's see you sit on your cloud and dream now.*

We talked about getting rid of the baby, but she couldn't, and I was real glad.

Brian Dance Alexander was born in Mount Sinai hospital on a cold-ass day in February. Lauryn's mother was so against me, she hadn't bothered to learn my last name was Dance, so when Lauryn slipped it in, her mom didn't even know what it meant. When I first saw him, all little with his skinny fingers spread out like he was showing off that he had five on each hand, I could feel my love for him swelling up inside of me. Lauryn was lying in the bed, her hair making a halo around her face against the pillow, smiling at me.

"If you're going to pick him up with your clumsy self," she said, "make sure you hold him over the bed."

I picked up my son, and it was like picking up what my life was supposed to be about. I really wanted to say something cool, something we would talk about down the road, but nothing came. I just held him and breathed in his smell and felt him moving in my arms as he was stretching himself out.

"Hey, little man," I said.

"Hey, Daddy," Lauryn said in a baby voice.

God, I loved that woman so much.

Then we slipped into a kind of dream, not a complete thing with pictures from magazines or talking about if the curtains in the living room should be the same color as the walls—not that kind of dream—but just talking to each other about what we were going to be doing. Like doing it was a done deal. Then her mama started talking to her about what she was going to do with the rest of her life.

"She said I got to think about the baby too," Lauryn said.

I didn't talk on the fact that her mama wasn't putting me in the picture. I was still hoping that things would come around somehow. Then her mama brought this older guy around and tried to hook him up with Lauryn. Her mom said he was a friend of hers from where she worked at the supermarket. But Lauryn peeped her program right away. She ran the whole thing down to me as we sat in Mickey D's down from the Magic Johnson theater on 125th Street.

"He's thirty-eight years old!" Lauryn was teary eyed and her lips were tight. "He come telling me he's from Barbados. As if I'm supposed to be impressed."

But Lauryn wasn't just mad, she was crying, and I knew that as foul as the crap her mother was putting out was, it made some kind of sense to her. The thing was that I didn't have no comeback except saying that the dude was old and that he had to be lame if he was wanting to hook up with a woman he didn't even know who had just had somebody else's baby. What I couldn't say was that I would take care of her better than he would.

What he had going on was he had a job. He managed the produce section in the supermarket.

I think, in my heart, that if Barbados boy had asked Lauryn to marry him right then and there, her mother would have said no. What that witch really wanted to do was to get me out of the picture.

"Hey, let's you and me get married and just see what happens," I said.

"Did you bring the ring?" she asked. She looked away.

I started to say that I didn't have a ring with me, but I knew she wasn't listening. She had thought it all through before we had met this time. She figured I might ask her to marry me, and knew I didn't have the money to buy a ring or hook up an apartment.

"So what you going to do?" I asked her when we reached her apartment.

"Keep on keeping on," she said. "Nothing else to do."

She was crying when she was going into the building. I remember saying good-bye to her after the door was closed.

I didn't want to do no dope. I just wanted to get myself together and take care of my business, but the shit was calling me again. When I hit the block, I knew what I was going to do. I copped two hits and took them home.

"You were good with Lauryn's crying?" Kelly asked.

"Yeah. I knew she was on edge, but I thought I could handle it," I said.

It used to be just when bad things happened that I needed some light, but it was getting to where when I seen good things going down,it was the life I wanted happening around me and me not getting to it that weighed on me, pushing me down into the dark hole that seemed like the only place I knew—sitting on the toilet cooking the hit and feeling sorry for myself.

"How you handle it?" Kelly asked.

I didn't like to shoot in my thigh because sometime it didn't take if you wasn't right in the line. I told myself

I needed some time to think, to clear the funk out my head so I could make a plan that was righteous for me and for Lauryn and the baby.

"How you handle it?" Kelly asked again.

How I'm going to tell you something when you can't understand it, man? You ain't been down where I live, how you gonna know what trying to get up means? How you gonna know that?

"How you handle it?" Kelly asked.

"I went to 125th Street and looked at some bassinets, because Lauryn said she wanted one for Brian. She said it had to be either white or blue.

"We have two models." The sales clerk looked Spanish. "This one is $64.99, and the one with the wheels is $84.99. Both come in pink, blue, or white, and both have wheels, but the $84.99 is expandable. So you don't have to lay out money for a crib in six months. Also, the mattress on the $84.99 is supposed to be better, but to me it doesn't make any difference. Babies like firm mattresses."

I told her I'd have to ask my wife and she said that was a good idea.

I had been thinking about showing up, knocking on the door, and then, when Lauryn's mother started talking about how I couldn't come into her house, just leaving the bassinet and walking away. Then I would know that Lauryn would be putting my baby into the bassinet I had bought for him. But I didn't have no $84.99 and I didn't have no $64.99. All I had was a lame excuse.

I went uptown to the corner. The usual dudes were there. I saw Skeeter and asked him how he was doing. He said he was doing all right. Skeeter was okay. He let me cop four bags for $35. He knew that sometimes you need a break.

"Yo, Lil J, why you doing drugs?" Kelly asked.

I looked over at him and he was still watching the television. On the screen I was in my building going up the stairs. I looked like an old man, pulling myself up like I was dead tired.

"You been hiding under a rock or something?" I asked Kelly. "You don't know why people use drugs?"

"I ain't talking about people," Kelly said.

"I'm talking about you. Or don't you even think about it?"

"No, I think about it. I think about it a lot. You know, some people go through life and all they got to carry is what they got in their pockets. They got a bill to pay, or they got some problem they need to make a decision on. It's not all that heavy. And what I got to carry ain't all that heavy either. But you know, I ain't got no strength. It's like everybody is stronger than me. So they pick up their load and move it at least a little. Me, I don't move it none, man."

"You moving it better when you high?" Kelly asked.

"No, but it don't weigh me down so much. When I come down off my high, I see I ain't been nowhere, ain't made no progress, and I just get ready to do it again."

KELLY TURNED DOWN THE VOLUME and I could hear the street sounds better. The tires made a hissing noise, and I thought it might be raining. I was hoping it was raining. Maybe everybody would just go home.

"So you want to change having the baby?" Kelly asked.

"What?"

"You talking about how bad the baby made you feel, right?" Kelly asked. "You wanted your girl-friend to get rid of it so you and her could just do what you needed to do."

"Don't be putting words in my mouth, man. If

I had a job, even a piece of a job like that fool her mama wanted her to hook up with . . ." I was still mad about her telling me I couldn't come into her house to see my son. "Maybe I would like to change the way Lauryn's mother treated me. If she had treated me decent, things might have worked out."

"How you gonna change what somebody else is thinking or what they do?" Kelly asked. "You talking about you didn't have a job, but the bottom line is you're the one that was—what you call it?—broke down?"

"Broke sick," I said. "Hey, get the television back on the street. You think they're going to search all the houses?"

"How I know?" Kelly looked at me like he was mad or something.

"You sitting there acting like you know so much," I said. "I should just kick your butt to see what you made of. You probably a punk."

Kelly giggled like a damn girl, and that got me mad. I told him not to be laughing at me. "I don't like people playing me."

"You want to get high?" Kelly asked.

"What you got?"

"Nothing," he said. "I just wanted to know if that was what you wanted. I know you get high when things don't go your way."

"You got a bathroom up in here?"

"Right down that hallway, left side," Kelly said.

The hallway was kind of dark, but I found the bathroom. It was one of those old bathrooms with a light on the side of a cabinet over the sink. I turned it on and closed the door. I was flat-out tired and feeling five kinds of terrible. My stomach was getting queasy, and my arm, which had been hurting on and off, was hurting even worse.

I just had to pee, but I was so tired I needed to sit down. When I went to undo my belt, I got a sharp pain in my arm. It made me want to cry. Not the pain, but just the way my whole thing was, like, falling apart. Some guys my age was away at college, or working or training in the army. Here I was in some tiny-butt bathroom trying to get my head together and rapping to some weird sucker that I didn't know what he was, let alone who he was.

Sitting on the little toilet with one arm shot up was stupid. I thought about what would happen if I heard the police running around outside. The Nine was still in my pocket, and I gripped it, but I couldn't use my left arm at all and I had to let the Nine go to get my johnson inside the toilet seat. It was like the whole world was clowning me.

When I finished peeing I got up, pulled my pants up, and noticed that my left wrist was swelling up. I thought maybe I was getting blood poisoning. If that happened, it didn't matter what the cops were doing, because I was going to die anyway or have to give myself up.

It come to me that maybe Kelly had a cell phone, and he could be calling the cops. Maybe he had even split. I started to run out, then just stood and leaned on the sink. It didn't make a difference anymore. Nothing was making a difference.

The cabinet over the sink had a mirror. One corner was messed up, as if maybe there had been a fire and it had got burned. I looked at myself in the mirror. My hair wasn't combed, my skin looked ashy, I looked ugly. Black and ugly.

I turned the light out and went back out toward the other room. Kelly was still sitting there, but I didn't know what he had been doing when I was in the bathroom.

"Hey, Kelly, you got a cell phone up in here?"

"Yeah, you got somebody to call?"

"No."

"Why don't you call your boy Maurice?" Kelly said. "See if he got that job?"

"He's asleep now," I said. "Anyway, I know he didn't get it."

"I think he got it," Kelly said.

He said it cold, like he knew what he was talking about. But it was more than that—it was like he was putting his mouth on me, saying I was definitely wrong for splitting from the line at Home Depot.

"I couldn't get that job," I said. "I didn't want Maurice to know it."

"Why couldn't you get it?" Kelly asked. Same voice. Flat. Cold.

"'Cause they check to see if you got a record, and I might have one," I said. "I'm not sure, but

Maurice is my boy and I didn't want him to know I been in jail."

"For selling drugs?"

"No, for trying to be somebody besides me," I said. "One time I was almost where I am now—"

"On this block?"

"No, man, don't be stupid," I said. "You know, not the outside of me, but inside. The way I feel and stuff, and the way things were going down. It was like, every way I turned, I was getting some heavy grief and I didn't see no way out of the situation. So, and this probably sounds a little stupid to you because you ain't into nothing, I decided to go down a different road. It was like, who I was—me—didn't have a way to make it. So I decided to be somebody else."

"Somebody else? How you going to do that?" Kelly turned and looked me up and down.

He hadn't really turned to me before, and where I was sitting I couldn't get a good look at him. But when he turned, I saw he was younger than I thought he was. That was a little disappointing. If he had been older, it would have been right that he knew stuff.

"That's just the way it was," I said. I was back in the chair. My arm hurt when I put it on the armrest. It was getting stiff, too. "Look, I ain't got no more time to waste with you."

"Yeah, you do," Kelly said.

I didn't know what he meant by that. I got up and went over to the window and pulled up the shade a little. There was only one police car and a dark van on the street.

"You thinking they waiting for daylight?" I asked.

"They probably waiting for you to show up," Kelly said. "But they don't know you in here, or else they would be coming in looking for you. So you might as well hang here until it's clear."

"I can't see the whole street from here," I said. "How I know if it's clear or not?"

"Maybe you can change something that will clear it up," Kelly said.

"I can't change nothing and neither can your dumb ass," I said.

"You just told me you wanted to change who you were," Kelly said. "Something about being somebody else and how it got you in jail. Didn't you say that?"

"I should cop some sleep," I said. "You don't know how tired I am."

"And everything is supposed to stop and wait for you to get some rest?" Kelly asked.

"Shut up."

We sat quiet for a long while. From the street I could hear car horns every once in a while. Kelly was kind of slouched down in his chair. I wondered how tall he was. He was thin, like me, and he sounded like he knew something about the street, but he was different, too.

When he was facing away from me, he looked regular, square shouldered, a little thin, not too strong. But when he moved, it was like I needed to pay attention, like something was going on. I thought of dudes who could play ball, who could lift their game into some other level that I didn't know about. That was Kelly, lifting his game even as we talked. I was hanging on. But I was afraid to let go.

I hadn't talked about trying to be a different

person before, but I had thought about it when I was down in Texas. I had thought about it and it made sense to me even though I didn't think it would make sense to anybody else. I wondered if Kelly could dig where I was coming from. He was changing a little. When I first got into the apartment, he was calm, and he seemed okay but not really friendly. Now he was getting irritated, like he wasn't really feeling me.

Sometimes I could put my thoughts into words and sometimes I couldn't. I thought if Kelly would ask me some questions, maybe I could answer them, but he wasn't asking.

"You know, right after it got really warm, in May, I got called down to the office in school," I started. "Mr. Trager, he's like an assistant principal, started running down my school record. He's all like, 'You're failing this and you're failing that,' and talking about how was I going to get on with my life and whatnot. I had heard all this before. I told Mr. Trager that he didn't know what my life was going to be like because he wasn't me. He didn't have no crystal ball to look into the future.

"To me this was same old same old. Some teacher or some principal talking me down and shaking his head or some woman teacher pushing my grades across the desk and asking me what I thought about them. And what I was saying to myself was the same thing I was saying to the people at the school. You know, just the way you could be sitting on the stoop and some suckers come flying down the street on a drive-by and waste you, or a brick could fall off the roof and kill you, something good could happen, too. Maybe you could hit the lottery or come up with a really great rap CD and go flashing through the rest of your life.

"People want to look at you and see your whole future laid out the way they know it, and I was saying that didn't happen. People aren't born with I'M GREAT! flashing on their foreheads. Anyway, when Mr. Trager gets down to the bottom line, he says to me that there wasn't any way that I was going to graduate. He started talking about how it wasn't the end of the world and that if I stayed in school another full year and worked hard, maybe I could graduate then.

"You know, that really messed with me. Because all the way up until then I was saying nobody could say this and that about what was going to happen, but now Mr. Trager was saying exactly what was going to go down. And when he said it—just laid it out like that—he was saying what I knew deep inside all the time."

"That you weren't going to graduate?" Kelly asked.

"No, more than that," I said. "I knew my program wasn't making it. You know, all these teachers be sitting in front of you talking like they're schooling you about where you are and where you're going, and you know better than they do. All you got to do is walk around and see what everybody who looks like you and lives around where you living is doing and see they just like you and they ain't going nowhere. And when you looking at television or seeing people who getting it on big-time and you see what they got going for them and then look at your hand and see you ain't got nothing, you know? That's the thing people can't see when they're explaining to your butt what's going on and how you messing up. They can't see that you knew it long before they did."

"And so what did you do?" Kelly asked.

"I said the hell with it," I said. "If I'm going to be pushed off the sidewalk, I might as well step on off. You know what I mean? Stop pretending something good was waiting around the corner and be what everybody expected me to be, which was another throwaway dude. So when Rico told me he was going down to Houston to see his cousin and asked me if I wanted to go with him, I said I'd go."

"You were down with Rico even before you and him got messed up with the cop thing?" Kelly asked.

"No, I didn't dig Rico at all because I knew he was foul," I said. "But if I was all mapped out to be foul, too, I might as well join the other side."

"Be somebody different?"

"Yeah. Because the old me was always hoping that things would work out while the new me was dealing with the truth. What threw it into gear was when he said he was going to Houston, which was the same week my class was graduating.

"What I found out was that there were a lot of guys not graduating. Some of them were going to the graduation and walking up on the stage like they were getting their diplomas, but all they got was an envelope with a note telling them to call the administrative office in three days. I found that out later."

"So you went to Houston?" Kelly asked.

"I went to Houston with Rico. We took the Hound from Port Authority and it took a while, but Rico had some dope he was taking down to Houston for a dealer. You know Rico, he's tapping all the way, snorting and drinking that energy drink and goofing on the other passengers. One of the drivers was hip to what we were doing and told us to get off his bus, so we had a two-day layover before we rolled into Houston.

"Meanwhile, I'm checking myself out because I had never used this much dope before. But I kept on telling myself that I didn't care. I knew I cared in a way, maybe even cared more than before, but back when I was telling myself that nobody knew what my life was going to be, I was telling myself that I didn't know the real deal about where my life was going and all."

"Riding that fantasy thing," Kelly said.

"Yeah. Maybe. I don't know. Maybe it was hope, or maybe one of those make-believe sets like you see in video games. You can make your own thing up. Anyway, we hit Houston and I was expecting something grand. Parts of the city were cool, but then you go to Chinatown—actually it's mostly Vietnamese—and then you get to their low-rent housing and it's the same as anyplace else. There's a lot of Mexicans in Houston, too. You ever been there?"

"Yeah."

"Then you know what I'm talking about," I said. "Rico's cousin put us up for a few days while Rico took care of his business. He picked up some nasty Brown Girl and actually mailed it back to New York, which I thought was cool."

"He mailed a girl back to New York?"

"No, a brick of brown heroin," I said. "That was what he was supposed to be in Houston for, to get some Brown Girl for Dusty. But then we ran out of money because Rico was shooting up all the stuff we had brought down to sell and lost a bunch of money gambling. Then he said we could do a stickup to get the money to fly back to New York. I was scared but I went for it."

"Why?"

"I guess I wanted to be like Rico," I said. "He was steady hustling and not worrying about nothing. If I could be like him, then it would be cool."

"Instead of being like you?"

"You slow, but you catch on after a while, right?"

Kelly smiled. I liked that. That was the first time I seen him smile, and I felt a little better. He didn't say nothing else for a while, and I thought maybe he was thinking he shouldn't have smiled. Sometimes when dudes smile a lot, people think they ain't hard enough to pull their weight and try to punk them out. I didn't want Kelly to think that I was like that, so I was running hard.

"So his boy, maybe it was his cousin, I don't know, told him about this little store we could hit on the highway," I said. "You know, when you get five minutes from downtown Houston, you ain't nowhere. I mean you ain't *nowhere.* They don't even have sidewalks in some of the places, and no buses or anything go there. You got to be driving."

"You drive?" Kelly asked.

"No, but this guy drove us and parked outside near the highway when we went in," I said. "The plan was that me and Rico was going to go in, with Rico pulling a thirty-eight he had borrowed to keep everybody covered while I took the money."

"And you just wrapped that around your head like it was nothing?" Kelly asked.

"I was nervous, but I was telling myself that I was hard enough to get over," I said. "I didn't want to be no thug, but I didn't see nothing else coming my way. It wasn't right or nothing, and I didn't want to hurt nobody, but . . . it was like being a thug and doing the thug thing was better than being me and standing on the corner with all the other beat-down dudes being thugged by the system."

"How much did you get?"Kelly asked.

"Nothing. Rico was high by the time we got in the place. I had snorted a quarter bag just to get my nerves together. I walked in first, and then Rico came in and had the gun down by his side," I said. "He must have had his finger on the trigger, 'cause soon as he walked up to the clerk it went off. *Bang!* There were two customers in the store and one of them was a cowboy or something. They say he messed with cattle. He punched Rico in the back of his head with his fist and Rico went down fast. The guy jumped on Rico and got the gun. At first I started easing toward the door, but I seen his cousin, who was scoping the whole deal through the window, take off in the car. I was the only other black dude in the store, and the guy behind the counter pulled a gun and pointed it at me.

"The cops came and got me and Rico and put us in the back of the police car. They asked us who we were and where we lived. I heard Rico give out some phony name and say he was from Chicago. I told them my name was Jimmy Alexander and I was from Chicago too. They took us down to the police station and put us in a cell with two Spanish dudes. They must have told them something, because as soon as the cops left the cell, they beat the crap out of us.

"I told them I was sixteen and Rico said he was nineteen. I got to go before a juvenile judge, and she asked me a bunch of questions about what I was doing with my life, and didn't I want to be a decent human being? I was real ashamed, but getting the beat-down told me right then and there that ain't nobody cared about how I was feeling. I got sentenced to a hundred and eighty days. I didn't know what was happening to Rico and I didn't care.

"They asked me a lot of questions about how I was brought up and whatnot, what my father was like. They told me I was a 'child in need of supervision' and I thought they might let me get into the wind instead of going to jail, but that wasn't going to happen."

"So you were in jail for six months?" Kelly asked.

"Unh-unh, for a hundred and twenty days, because I got some time off for good behavior. They don't play in Houston. You do what they say and when they say it. Every time you walk outside your cell, you got to have your hands behind your back like you handcuffed even though you're not," I said. "And the dudes in the center—man, you got some lowlife people in them jails. A lot of gangbangers thinking they maybe should shank you to make their reps, or shank you because they think you said something that disrespected their gang, or maybe slice you in your face just to break up the day.

"You know, they say that juvenile centers ain't as bad as an adult prison, but it was bad to me. What they do, the way they treat you, you don't feel like a people, I mean like a person. That sounds stupid, huh?"

"How did you feel?"

"You feel like . . . you could be like an animal or something. Because when you're a person, you can do something that you want to do. Maybe you can't do everything, but you can do some things. And you think about it, an animal—say he a pet or something—got to eat what his owner put down on the floor. And that's what we had to do. We had to eat what they give us. We got franks and beans and a lot of green snap beans, which I don't like, and a lot of Jell-O and cereal and eggs. You could be hungry at the center but you didn't look forward to eating. You could be tired, but you didn't want to lie down on that bunk they gave you.

"Before I went there, I had thought about what I wanted to be. You know, it was like a future thing—but they take all that out of you," I said. "What you start thinking about is what you is—what you *are.* What I'm saying is that if you're a human being, that's supposed to mean something. I mean something different from a dog or a cat or a rock. But sitting in that cell—they called it 'quarters,' but it was a cell—I was thinking on what I was and how I wasn't a dog. You hearing me?"

"I'm hearing you," Kelly said.

"When I got out, I was on the same bus coming back into Houston with this white girl from Harrisburg, Pennsylvania. She said her name was Sabrina, but after a while I didn't believe anything she said. She was like one of those white girls you see on television been abused. She was real smart, she could have been a doctor or something, because when we got back into Houston, she showed me how she could walk into a drugstore and steal stuff to get high on right off the counter. She knew the name of everything they had in the drugstore and how to fix it up to get a buzz. One time she even took me into a grocery store and got some nutmeg and we messed with that."

"You liked her."

"No, I wasn't feeling her, but I could see where she was coming from," I said. "The drugs were putting her in another place. She didn't need to think about what was really on her mind. Plus she taught me a lot of stuff. She could look you dead in your eyes and be robbing you blind at the same time. She didn't mean to be so cold, but that's the way it turned out for her. She taught me how to cop from drugstores—mostly pain medicine and stuff for colds—and how to use it to string out your jones so you could handle it.

"Sabrina was okay. Kind of like me, feeling throwed away, and her being throwed away and us seeing each other and knowing what was going down. It's like you ain't in the world everybody is talking about, the one they got on television and in the newspapers. You in another world where you ain't supposed to get over, you just lucky if you get by.

"We hitchhiked together until we reached Pennsylvania; then she went her way knowing I was out there keeping on keeping on, and I kept going my way knowing the same thing until I got back to Harlem."

"YO, KELLY, YOU WATCHING the street?"

Kelly got the television back onto the street. I tried to watch how he did it, but he was too quick. We looked at the monitor, and there was still just one police car and a van.

"Then what happened?" Kelly asked. "After you got back to Harlem?"

"Kelly, why you got this setup?" I asked. "What you into? You a cop or something, right?"

"How's your arm? You haven't been mentioning it lately," Kelly said.

I hadn't been thinking about my arm, but soon

as Kelly asked me, I kind of grabbed it. It wasn't hurting. My fingers moved good when I wiggled them, and the swelling was down some.

"Hey, Kelly?"

"What?"

"I'm a little scared of you," I said. "You know that?"

"You scared of everything you don't know about, right?" he said.

"I guess."

"You just getting in deeper and deeper, huh?" Kelly hunched his shoulders and rubbed the back of his neck like he was getting tired.

"I wasn't trying to," I said. "It's like a old movie I saw one time. It was hot and I couldn't sleep and I put the television on and this flick come on about people looking for gold in Africa. Something like that. One guy fell into some quicksand. As long as he didn't move around, he went down slow. Soon as he got to move, he started going down faster. That's how I feel sometimes."

"Sound like you feeling sorry for yourself," Kelly said.

"Hey, I'm the one in this skin looking out," I said. "I might be feeling sorry for myself the way you said, but I'm the one being messed over, right?"

"Ain't you messing over yourself?"

"Does it matter? Does it really matter if it's some white dude downtown or some brother on the corner or me all by myself if the result is the same?" I asked. "Does it really matter?"

"Yeah, it does," Kelly said, looking away from me. "'Cause if it's somebody who ain't in your skin, you don't feel the punches when you fight back."

"Whatever. You think it's going to be safe for me to split once it gets light?" I asked.

"It won't be light for a while," Kelly said. "Go on with your story."

I didn't feel like going on with it. Kelly was right when he said I was feeling sorry for myself. I knew that. That's why it was better sometimes just not to feel anything. I didn't know why he wanted me to go on, either, but he did.

"When I got back to Harlem, I fell into my old place. My moms was glad to see me, but she was looking bad, stringy and skinny. She asked me where I had been and all, but she wasn't acting like she was missing me, more like she was mad that I wasn't there. She was coughing and spitting up stuff. It was kind of disgusting. She was on Medicaid and taking all kinds of pills. I scoped her pills, and from what Sabrina had taught me, I knew I could get a buzz on from what she had. She had them time-release capsules, and I took them apart and cooked them up and went for the line. I didn't worry about OD'ing on painkillers, so that's why I went for the line instead of just skin popping.

"I looked for a job and got back into the same old routine. Once in a while I found some pickup work. They started a new company where you go to this office and they send you out here and there to work. Whoever you working for don't pay you, they pay the company and then the company pays you. It's crappy, but it's some pocket change.

"I could also sell some of my mom's pills downtown on Forty-Deuce. Sometimes on Sundays when there was a football game, you could sell pills to the guys going to the game. I guess they go over there and drink they beer and take some pills and enjoy themselves. You could sell more pills when the Jets were playing than when the Giants were playing. That was funny, but everybody knew it."

"Your mama know you left tonight?"

"No."

"You want to call her?" Kelly asked.

"You got a . . . ? Yeah, you do. No, I don't want to call her. I don't know what to say to her."

"She might like to hear from you," Kelly said. He handed me a cell phone.

I wanted to peep Kelly's faves in case he was a cop. He could have had Homicide or Detectives listed. I didn't, because the brother had me scared. I dialed home and waited for four rings before I heard Mom's voice.

"Hello?"

"Yo, Moms, me, Lil J."

"Where you at? The police been in here looking for you. You didn't shoot no cop, did you?"

"No, but I got to get my stuff together so I can prove it," I said. "How you doing?"

"Boy, my nerves is gone! Those cops were so nasty. They tore up the place looking for you. Took all my dishes out the cabinet and put them on the floor. Now how you going to be in there?"

"Don't worry," I said. "I'll be all right."

"Where are you now?"

"I'm at a friend's house, but I can't tell you where."

"One of the detectives gave me a card with a number to call so you can give yourself up," Moms said. "But I don't trust them cops. I think you should wait until you can get you a lawyer to go to the police station with."

"You hear anything about the cop?" I asked.

"You mean the one that was shot?"

"Yeah."

"They had his wife on television talking about how they needed to get the animals off the street," Moms said. "What's your number so I can call you back?"

"I got to go," I said. "I'll call you later."

I hung up the phone.

We didn't have nothing to say for a while, and

then I realized my arm was beginning to hurt again. This time the pain got bad faster than before.

"Kelly, what you think is going to happen if I just give myself up?" I asked.

"You mean, just give up and be like Rico?" he asked.

"What? No, I mean give myself up to the police."

"You'll think about it for a while," Kelly said. "Then you'll remember what it was like at the juvenile center, and what everybody said jail was like and how long twenty-five years is. . . ."

On the screen I saw myself on the roof landing again. I saw my face all twisted up and ugly and I saw myself lifting the Nine to my head.

"Yo! Stop it! Stop it! *Please!*" I was begging him. "Please stop it, Kelly. Run it back some more, man. Please."

"Where you want me to run it back to now?" Kelly asked.

"Did I tell you I was a rapper?" I asked. I was scared and shaking. "I was rapping strong, Kelly. I could really rhyme."

There's two kinds of rules
Rules for the man
And rules for the fools
The rules for the fools ain't nothing but tools
To lock away the black man's mind
So when he finds he down with a frown
Looking up from the gutter
All he can do is stutter and thinking
That's where he belongs and stinking
Like a piece of week-old meat
In the super ghetto of defeat
And when he fails to make bail
And ends up in jail with homies for roomies

Rhyming "doing the time"
With "doing the crime"
He's figuring that's the ghetto theme
Instead of a scheme
Punk-tuated in some light bling-bling
And the same old thing except the
Chains is nine-karat gold
And the brother's been told
They about bravery instead of slavery
So when the brother comes in stumbling
and humbling
He thinks he's getting a fair deal
While the real deal is that he's just getting the fare
To whatever lockdown need some new bodies.
But the game is over
'Cause Cellblock Four is taking over
And just like these words are being spoken
We know the rules are made to be broken
Yeah, yeah, the game is over!

They don't want us to use the N-word
So we'll be the triggers, but know what we mean
'Cause we'll be on the scene

Shooting off more than our mouths
From north to south
And when the judge turn the pages
We go into rages 'cause his statutes and laws
Don't do nothing but put justice on pause
We got a whole nation behind bars
And a few who loose and think they stars
'Cause some other brother holding their number
While they out here in the world of slumber
Talking about some law and order
While the Man slipping dope across the border
But the game is over
'Cause Cellblock Four is taking over
And just like these words are being spoken
We know the rules are made to be broken
Yeah, yeah, the game is over!

"What you think?" I asked Kelly.

"It's okay," Kelly said. "I like rap. How come you didn't go on with it?"

"Why don't you run my group on your television?" I said. "Check it out for yourself?"

Kelly was keeping the remote in his hand. He

lifted it and pointed it toward the television. I was getting better at recognizing where I was and peeped the school media center.

"Yo, man, you know Miss Oglivie won't go for that,"Omar said, leaning back in the lounge chair, and shook his head. "She said we could have a rap group, but everything had to be positive. That's the whole purpose of the group."

"Yeah, how are we going to have a positive rap group called Cellblock Four?" Victor asked. He was Omar's cut buddy, so I knew he was going to back him up.

"What's positive for one person don't have to be positive for everybody," I said. "You trying to be positive or you trying to suck up?"

"Here's what the story is," said Deon Crooms, who was sitting across from us at a little card table. He spoke in a low voice. "Miss Oglivie came to us with the idea of putting together a rap group, and she told us what she wanted. It was supposed to be about taking care of business in school, getting your life together, that kind of thing. If that's what she wants, she's not going to be going for something about being thugs."

"He's right and you know it," Omar said.

"Who wants to hear that stuff except Miss I-Wish-the-Hell-I-Was-White Oglivie and some junior Uncle Tom wannabes?" I said. "People want to hear about some dudes getting hard and standing up to the power. What you think all them OG's is about?"

"I'm not some Uncle Tom and I'm as black as you'll ever be," Deon said. "But I'm sick of hearing about black men having to be gangsters and getting shot forty-five times so they can say they keeping it real."

Deon was looking around the room like he had said something deep and was grooving on it.

"So what you saying?" I asked Deon. "You saying that we're supposed to be rappers, but somebody else is going to dictate the rhymes and all we're going to do is follow the program?"

"Why can't you think positive?" Omar asked. "How are you different? What you saying ain't nobody heard?"

"Getting your head together isn't positive?" I asked.

"I don't think you can think of nothing positive," Deon came back. "What you talking about sounds weak to me."

Deon played a little ball and was believing he was all that and then some. He had been making some bad noise in my direction for a while. He had his head to one side, eyeballing me like I was short or maybe didn't have the heart to step to him.

"Check this out, Deon." I went over to where he was sitting and pulled up a chair right in front of him. "I think you're weak. What's more, I think you need for somebody to do a serious readjustment of your thinking patterns by slamming you upside your head. What I'm thinking is maybe if I knock one of your ears clean through your head, it'll filter out all them turds you got in your brain that you calling ideas."

I could look into his eyes and see he didn't know what to say. He had built up his front like a true mind warrior, but when the deal was on the table his heart was skipping beats.

"I think you're going to throw away the whole deal," he said. "Instead of a rap group we gonna end up with nothing."

"We're going to be blowing a free period and everything," I heard Omar saying from behind me.

"Let's have a vote on it," Victor said.

"You vote on it," I said, standing up. "I got things to do."

I was hot when I left the lounge.

We were in an assembly when Miss Oglivie first suggested that we start a rap group. I was down with the program, but as soon as she started talking about "positive values" and all that crap I knew she didn't mean nothing good. She picked Omar and Victor, and Deon volunteered. A girl we called Silly threw in my name, but I knew that it was Lauryn, who I was getting real serious with, who had told her to do it. A lot of kids gave me a cheer because I had made a smoking rhyme about a brother who got killed on 125th and Park under that little railroad bridge that goes into Grand Central Station. Maurice, my ace, had dug it and asked me to do it on tape over a reggae beat. I did it and he burned a bunch of copies on CDs and we passed them around, so they knew I was strong.

Miss Oglivie didn't like it, but she had to take me. Omar, Victor, and Deon stuck together like the lames they were, and I knew a vote was going to go against me.

After school I saw Lauryn on Lenox Avenue. For a change she wasn't with Silly. I had just got some fresh minutes on my cell and called her. We were walking downtown, me on one side of the street and her on the other side.

"I heard you and Deon almost got into it," she said.

"No, he don't want me," I said. "All he wants is to run his mouth."

"It's still about naming the group?" she asked.

They had wanted to call the group The Righteous Brothers, which was definitely up there and I would have gone along with it if the raps they were running were good. But they were just catching words from Miss Oglivie and snatching slogans off the wall and laying them out like they were something somebody wanted to be hearing.

"It's not just about the name," I said. "It's about the whole set, same as it was before."

"Where you going?" Lauryn asked.

"Thought I'd check out Milbank," I said. "See if anybody's over there." I was really going to the brownstone man, but I didn't want to tell Lauryn that because she didn't want me using anything.

"Why don't you come over to my place and check me out?" she said.

"I thought you and Silly were supposed to be doing something," I said.

"So you saying that you don't want to see me?" she asked.

"I'm just saying that—" I looked over to where she was and saw that she had stopped walking. "I'm just saying that after all the grief I had today, I need to relax a little. Thought maybe I would hoop a little."

"Lil J, you going to cop?" Right up front.

"No," I lied. "I'm just tense, that's all."

"So why don't you cop and then come over to my house?" she said. "Do it in front of me. Why you slipping and sliding?"

"I told you I wasn't going to cop," I said.

"Why you shouting into the phone?" she came back.

"So what you want?" I asked. It even sounded weak to me.

"Stay there," she said. "I'll go with you to get the stuff."

Lauryn was treating me like I was a stone head, but I knew I wasn't. I could let the shit go in a heartbeat, but I just wasn't ready to go, not just yet, and she couldn't get next to that. But I knew where she was coming from, because I had seen a lot of dudes who thought they just had chippies and they was drowning and looking for the big fish to come save their butts but the big fish wasn't coming. My roll was different. I was correct and knew where I was going, and that was the truth—only it didn't sound so good when I wasn't shouting it. When I was just saying it to myself, it didn't sound too good at all.

I appreciated where Lauryn was coming from. She was steady in my corner and I knew it.

I saw her coming across the street. She was looking good, as usual. What she didn't know was that I was as tense as I told her I was. She thought I was just out to party a little. But all that crap with the rap group was getting me down, and I didn't feel like going home and dealing with my moms. Lauryn came up to me and I could see she was wearing her attitude.

"I did think you were going to be hanging out with Silly," I said.

"It's nice of you to be concerned about her," Lauryn said.

Silly was the best-looking woman in the whole world. Her real name was Alicia, but all the guys started calling her Silly because that's the way she made you feel when she came around and you didn't know where to put your eyes. Alicia and

Lauryn were probably the smartest students in the school, too. Silly was thinking about being either a historian or a dancer, and Lauryn wanted to be a lawyer. They were both serious about their lives.

"So what you want to do?" I asked.

"You were going to cop, so let's go do it," Lauryn said.

We had some more back-and-forth, and at first I figured she thought I'd be too shamed to use in front of her. Then she was insisting and my head was tilting to maybe she wanted to party.

The brownstone man was on 105th and Park. He ran a little bodega on the corner and sold stuff from Mexico right over the counter. I knew the cops had to be on to him, but he was always open for business. Lauryn waited outside for me while I went in, bought two hits and a bag of chips, and came out.

We didn't talk on the train uptown on the way to her house.

Lauryn's parents were separated. Her mother had a good gig and did all the right things. She went with Lauryn to museums and plays and saw to it that Lauryn always had some cash and dressed good. Lauryn was a day and a half past fine and knew how to present herself.

The apartment was clean and everything was in its place. It wasn't like my pad, with a sink full of dirty dishes and little armies of empty plastic medicine bottles all over the place.

"So you tense, go on and get untense," Lauryn said.

"So what you saying?" I asked.

"What am *I* saying?" Lauryn put her palms up. "I'm not saying anything. I'm just sitting here at my kitchen table waiting for you to get yourself untense. You're the one that's running the show."

"Hey, Lauryn, let me get to the bottom line," I said.

"You going to snort the line or shoot it up?"

That shut me up, and I didn't know what to say to her. I just sat there for a long time with my head down. Then I was hearing her on the screen and at the same time I wasn't hearing her, because I was trying to shut it out. I asked Kelly to shut the television off.

"You dope up in front of her?" Kelly asked.

I nodded. "Just turn it off."

"Why, don't you think it's time to see what you been doing?"Kelly asked. "How you going to put some reason to it if you keep running away from the set?"

"I wasn't running away from nothing. Sometimes it was like the heroin calling to me. When I didn't have nothing, I could think about giving it up, about turning away and doing something else. Sometimes, when I really wanted to party and didn't have the money, I'd go play some ball or just watch television and the feeling would go away. But when I had money, or when I had already scored a hit, I got nervous. I didn't have to have the dope, but when I had it, I had to use it. You know what I mean?"

"No," Kelly said. "Let me watch the screen."

Lauryn's mom kept aluminum foil in a cupboard, and I saw myself getting it. I folded it up into a little upside-down tent and put the hit in the middle of it. I didn't look at Lauryn as I heated it up over the front burner on the stove and watched it melt. I watched myself changing hands as the foil got hot, then watched the hit steam up.

I didn't dig the smell as I breathed it in deep, and my throat was feeling bad in a heartbeat.

I was saying something to Lauryn, but she didn't answer. Sitting with Kelly, I didn't remember what I had said.

I told myself I was going to be cool as the dragon found a comfortable place in my body. I could feel it shifting and moving and finding places that needed chilling out. I put the foil down in a cigarette tray when it was done.

Kelly turned the sound back up and I told him to shut it off. He said no.

"So tell me about this great love you feeling for me," Lauryn said. "Now that you're not tense anymore."

"It's true," I said. "You're like a bridge in my life."

"That is so tired, Lil J," Lauryn said. "Men have

been talking about women being bridges in their lives for umpteen years. Far as I'm concerned, a bridge is just something you walk on to get someplace else. Is that what I am to you? Something you can walk on as you move to your next high?"

"No, I mean, like—there's two worlds. There's the world you see in the newspaper. You know, important stuff going on. People in their business suits rushing around to meetings or talking about how this thing or that thing is going to affect the world," I said. "They're like the real people, because that's all you be reading about in the papers or seeing on television. When they kick out the news every night, that's who they're talking about. And then there's . . ."

The hit was rising fast and I was holding on, trying to pay attention.

"Then there's the world I live in," I said. "People ain't doing nothing. Walk down the street and brothers just standing and leaning against whatever. Passing time. Or maybe time passing them. I don't know."

"I think I'm pregnant," she said.

"What?"

"That wasn't the right answer," she said.

My mouth was fuzzy dry and my brain was running around trying to find a landing place.

"Yo, I love you, and I'm going to be there for you. . . ." The words didn't have any weight. They were just coming out my mouth and floating away.

Lauryn was crying.

Me and Kelly sitting in the dark, the room getting cold, and on the screen was this picture of Lauryn looking all alone. And then there was the sound of her crying. The crying filled the screen, and filled the corners of the room with me and Kelly, and filled all the dark places in the world.

The camera was on my face. My lips were moving.

"I love you, Lauryn," I said.

"You left the burner on," she said.

"SO YOU CUT LAURYN LOOSE?" Kelly asked.

"In a way, because I was still using," I said. "But she didn't cut me loose. She's good that way. I wanted to get straight, but I needed some time. You know, when you getting ready to have a kid, you want to get your act together. I guess I just needed more time."

"Seem to me all you got is time," Kelly said. "What you need more time for?"

"I can't explain it, man," I said. "You got to live it to give it. You ain't been in my shoes, you don't know where I'm coming from."

"No, I know where you coming from." Kelly

sniffed, then cleared his throat. "You just got some stink on yourself and don't want to deal with it. You got a woman. You got a baby. You breathing twenty-four/seven, but you needing something different to deal with."

"You don't know that."

"Then why don't you run it by me so I can understand it," Kelly said.

"Maybe I don't feel like it," I said.

"Yeah, maybe you don't. But you know what? You seen yourself upstairs on the roof with the piece in your hand," Kelly said. "You going to unknow that? Like you unknowing what's going down with Lauryn? Like you unknowing what's going down with Brian?"

"Run what by you?"

"Run down what dope doing for you," Kelly said.

"Maybe you said it right the first time," I said. "Maybe what it's about is, I don't want to know what I'm about. I don't see nothing ahead for me. I don't see nothing coming down the road—no car saying, *Get on in, I'll give you a lift*. Maybe I don't want to deal with that. You know, I ain't the first guy like me I've seen. You see guys like me all the time in the 'hood. Nodding out and feeling the same way I feel. Going from day to day until it's over and somebody making chalk marks around their bodies or they're sitting in a cell someplace. What about that I need to know more than I know now?"

"How about the rap group?" Kelly asked. "You weren't that bad."

"Omar, Victor, and Deon went on with it and I laid low," I said. "There was going to be an assembly and they were supposed to do a presentation. It was like jive from the get-go and everybody knew it was going to be. Maurice hooked me up with a portable amplifier and a speaker and I had an idea I was going to let them do their thing on the stage and then I was going to come from the back and make a challenge. I figured I would blow the place up with my rhymes because they were tough and they weren't pulling any punches.

"I know this white boy named Ryan who hung out with the brothers, and he had his own amp and stuff. He was kind of lame, but he knew all the jams and he could lay down a beat with his mouth. You know, he would make sounds like he was scratching and then throw in some scat with it. If you just heard him and didn't see him, you would think he was from Jamaica or someplace. Anyway, he was going to come down the side while I came down the middle aisle. We figured everybody would turn and check us out and then the guys onstage would have to deal with it.

"Omar and them went on first, and they put out some garbage that was even worse than I thought it was going to be. They couldn't even keep a beat. When they went through their first set, Miss Oglivie stood up and started talking about giving them a big hand. That's when me and Ryan started up. Just like I thought, everybody got into what we were doing right away. They were showing us instant love, but Miss Oglivie stopped the whole show. 'Everybody sit down! Everybody sit down!' Then she told me and Ryan to leave the auditorium. That was it. A lot of people came over to me later and said we were on the money, but it didn't make no never-mind. Miss Oglivie threw away our thing.

"We got called down to the principal's office and everything, but it didn't matter. Nobody really cared about anything. They didn't care about what me and Ryan did, they didn't care about Omar and them. They were just talking about ordering sandwiches for a meeting."

There was the sound of a siren outside the window. I looked toward the window and then pointed at the screen. Kelly looked over at me and then clicked the remote, and we were looking at a different view of the street. Another black-and-white had pulled up. Its lights were flashing and the siren was going.

"Something's up!" I said.

"I don't think so," Kelly said. "They're just sounding their siren to see who comes to the window."

I was almost at the window and stopped. "You ever run from the police?" I asked.

"No, but I'm not scared," Kelly said. "I'm thinking straight. You scared and you're hurting."

"You ever been hurt?" I asked. "I mean, really hurt?"

Kelly put his head down and glanced at me out the corner of his eye. "Yeah, I've been hurt."

"Shot?"

"No."

"You ain't been hurt unless you been shot," I said.

"Yeah, you're all world now, huh?" Kelly said. "You can go around bragging on being shot. But pain isn't all that bad. People learn to deal with pain. People get cancer. People get shot up in wars and blown up a lot worse than you. They learn to deal with it."

I wanted to go back to the window. I asked Kelly if he was sure there wasn't anything happening outside. He said he wasn't sure.

"You think I'm going to be okay?" I asked him.

"I guess it depends on what you mean by okay," he said. "Everything you telling me sounds like you haven't been okay in a long time. You don't know what to go back and change."

"How you going to *change* something that happened in the past anyway?" I asked. "That don't make any sense."

"So let's go on to the future," Kelly said.

I saw the screen flicker and there I was, sliding up the stairs to the roof landing. I knew what was going to come next.

"Hey, Kelly, stop it," I said. "Yo, man, what's wrong with you?"

He stopped the screen image, but I couldn't take my eyes off the still picture. I was half standing, half crouched over. I saw the Nine still in my hand. I looked up at my face. My eyes were like something wild.

I thought I saw the image move and I started to ask Kelly not to let it run, but then I saw it wasn't moving. It was the image in my head that was still going. I was remembering what I had seen before. It was like a nightmare I could see with my eyes open.

"Breathe," Kelly said.

I didn't notice I had been holding my breath.

The pain in my arm was getting worse.

"Kelly, I ain't doing too good getting rid of this pain," I said.

"Yeah, I see that," Kelly said.

"You know, the worst pain I ever had, I didn't even feel it?" I said. "I woke up in the middle of the night and I was like—all crying and shit—and I don't know why. I didn't have a bad dream and I hadn't even gone to bed sad. But I woke up crying like anything. That got me so down, I didn't want to get out of bed. I still don't know why that happened."

"You deeper into your jones than you want to talk about?" Kelly said. "How long you been tracking?"

"Too long."

"Thought you were scared of needles?"

"It moves you away from yourself quick," I said. "I know it's foul, but that's where I'm at. Can you get the picture back on the street?"

Kelly clicked the picture, and we were looking at the street again. It had started to rain. One police car was still parked under the streetlight.

Through the glass I could see two figures. They weren't clear, just sitting in the front seat. Every so often the wiper swept across the windshield, and for a tiny moment I could see the policemen inside. I wondered what they were talking about, if they were hating me.

"You think that cop is going to live?" I asked.

"How I know?"

"What you think?"

Kelly just shrugged.

I wanted to hear me talking or Kelly talking or even a car passing on the street. Anything but the silence. I tried to think of what I wanted to change in my life, to go back and get something that Kelly could dig on. That's what I wanted to do. It was like he had a way of understanding me and looking inside of me that made me feel good. No, not good, just that he understood. He was right in saying I was trying to unknow things about myself, things that I hadn't told anybody before. Some of the things I had heard people say about me. Lauryn had said some of them. But there were things that I wasn't sure about. Like if I liked myself the way I hoped other people would like me, like I was trying to get Kelly to like me.

"Hey, Kelly, you ever hide what you doing?" I asked. "Like you don't want anybody to peep your hole card?"

"I guess so," Kelly said. "Sometimes. You hiding something?"

"You were talking about me not wanting to know things, but I got more things I don't want other people knowing," I said. "I got some stuff in me that I don't even tell Lauryn."

"Sometimes you don't have to tell people," Kelly said. "They already understand where you coming from."

"No, she don't know how scared I get sometimes. You know I'm up in here and I'm scared because the police are looking for me," I said. "But sometimes I'm just scared to walk down the street. I ain't afraid of being shot or anything, I'm just afraid. You understand that?"

"I understand you feeling it," Kelly said. "You see what you doing to yourself, you figure you got to be afraid of something."

"I think my moms is scared too. When I was thirteen things really got bad for us. She started hitting the bottle hard. At first she would go out and get her a bottle of rum and bring it home. I didn't like that because we didn't have money for anything. We'd get some money on our family card and she would cash part of it in for money to buy liquor. That's a street hustle.

"Then she started hanging out half the night. One time I was home and a neighbor came to the door and said my moms was downstairs in the hallway. She said she looked sick. I rushed downstairs and she wasn't sick, just drunk. When she wasn't drinking, she was depressed. Sometimes she said she had pains in her stomach, but I think mostly she was depressed. If I got up late at night to go to the bathroom, I would find her sitting at the kitchen table in the dark. I'd ask her what she was thinking about and she'd say, 'Nothing.' When I started messing up in school and they asked me what was wrong, I said the same thing. 'Nothing.'"

"SO YOU WANT TO CHANGE what happened to you in school?" Kelly asked.

"It wasn't real enough to change," I said. "School is like a dream that's going on, and it's good and everything, but it ain't going on about you. That's the way it was for me, anyway. I was supposed to be filling my head up with what they were teaching, but it didn't go down that way."

"Nobody gave you the right information?"

"They give me the right information, or it was right as far as I was concerned, but I wasn't hopping around passing out high fives or nothing,"

I said. "It was like I was knowing two different things. One was like school is smoking and your trip to the big time, but the other thing was that hey, it didn't do nothing for people I knew. Can you get my school on the television?"

"Is it strong enough in your mind?" Kelly asked.

"It got to be strong in my mind to get it on television? You never said that before."

"Is it strong enough?"

"I think so," I said. "Check it out."

Kelly started with his remote again and had me thinking about how strong school was on my mind. I was wondering if he really meant that it had to be strong or if he was just messing with me.

I watched as the television focused on the hallway in the first floor of Carver High. Then I saw me sitting in the office, but I was younger. I leaned forward and took a look at myself. My face was rounder on the bottom. I had on my light brown sweater and my fly Nikes and I was looking good.

"How old are you again, Jeremy?" All the kids

at Carver High knew that when Mr. Lyons took off his jacket, he was serious. He had his jacket off as I sat in his office.

"Thirteen," I said.

"Jeremy, why don't you look over your test scores and tell me what you think about them." He pushed a long sheet of paper in front of me.

Why didn't he just go ahead and tell me I messed up? That's what the meeting was all about. He knew what the scores were like. Why did we have to go through all the gaming?

"You were doing fairly well in math before," he said. "I think you were at grade level, weren't you?"

"Yes."

"So what's been happening this year?"

"Nothing."

"Nothing?" He leaned back in his chair like he was expecting a different answer.

He was talking and I was looking down at the sheet with the test scores. They had circles around the bad marks. Almost all the kids in my class have been called down for this same jive talk. What happened? Why didn't you do better?

I was sitting in the classroom and my head was filled up and I couldn't get no more in it.

"What's going on in your life to make your test scores fall like this?" His voice was okay, like he wasn't trying to put me down.

Yesterday—was it yesterday or the day before yesterday? The days run together—I was home and Mrs. Burnett came to my door and said my mother was down in the hallway and she looked sick. I ran downstairs and saw her lying in the hallway. Her dress was up around her thighs and I pulled it down.

"Mama! Mama!" I called to her and she moved a little. I could smell her breath and it was stinking. "Mama! Get up!"

She was heavy, but I pulled her up. No, she wasn't heavy, just kind of limp. I didn't want nobody else to see her like this. When we got to the stairs, I tried to get her arm over the banister. Mr. Alston came out his house, and when he saw us on the stairway he just stood there a minute and looked. He asked me if I needed any help, and I told him to get the hell back into his own apartment.

He didn't move and I kept trying to get Mama up the stairs.

Mr. Alston told me to get on the inside and put one arm around her waist and hold on to the banister to pull myself up. He steadied her while I changed positions. I was crying a little because I was ashamed for him to see us like this. Two more people passed us on the stairway. One woman said something about wasn't it a shame the way people carried themselves. I wanted to punch her in her face.

I got Mama up to our floor and then put my hands under her shoulders and dragged her down the hall. Once I got her into the apartment, I just left her there, lying on the kitchen floor. I started thinking about who she had been drinking with, and what she had been doing. I felt mad and sorry at the same time. I wasn't sorry for her, either. I was sorry for me.

"You know there aren't a lot of young black men

with good math skills." Mr. Lyons was still talking. Still saying what I should be doing and how important school was.

What did I look like to him? Did I look like I was just a retard who couldn't figure out what school was about? He could shut up and I could give his whole rap right back to him the same as he was giving it to me. What would I say?

"Jeremy, school is the most important thing in your life. If you don't go to school, you're just going to be like all those other black guys hanging around wasting your time and getting in trouble. You can't get a good job without a good education. You need to read to succeed. You can be anything you want to be. You just need to make up your mind that you want to be somebody. Your future is in your hands! Jeremy, if you don't get yourself together you will be sorry."

I watched television in my room for a while. There was a movie on, but all I could see in my head was Mama drinking with some men on the corner. Even though I hadn't seen her do that, I knew what some of the men did to women when they were high.

There wasn't anything in the refrigerator that looked good. Some leftover stew. Some franks and beans we had had the night before. I knew she hadn't eaten anything. I remembered a program I had seen about a man choking on a hot dog. I didn't want her to choke, so I ate the franks and beans. I was going to warm them up, but cold was just as good.

I had to step over her to get to my bedroom.

When I got up in the morning, she was in the bathroom. I saw she had made tea and the water was still warm. I had tea and oatmeal. She came out the bathroom and asked me why I hadn't left for school.

I looked at the clock and it was still early. Then she asked me why I wasn't home when she got home last night.

She didn't remember! She didn't even remember lying in the hallway, nothing! I wanted her to feel bad, to say she was sorry. I wanted her to look away when I walked into the room. Instead, she didn't remember a thing.

She asked me where I had been again, and I said I had been out playing ball.

"You win?" she asked.

"No," I said. "I lost."

My Sunday shirt was the only clean one, and I wore that. She said I looked good. She smiled when she said it. She had a nice smile when she was sober.

I went to the bathroom and saw her pills on the sink. One bottle was for her rash and the other one was for her nerves. I took two of her nerve pills.

English was my first class and the teacher didn't call on me.

Math was my second class. Miss Callie was talking about square roots. Her mouth was moving and words were coming out and I could hear them as they floated across the classroom, but none of them was sticking in my head. It was like Miss Callie was talking English but I wasn't understanding it. Or maybe like calling your friend and he's not home and having the voicemail say that there was no room for messages. That's what my head was like, no room for messages.

"Is there something bothering you, Jeremy?"

What was I going to say? Tell him the best way to carry your mother up the stairs was to put one arm around her waist and pull yourself up along the banister? The best way to get her up off the floor was to pull her by her shoulders until you got her sitting up, then get behind her and lift her and hope she didn't fall on her face? *Uhn-uhn.* I ain't going there. You can't do nothing about it, so why do I need to go there? So you can feel sorry for me or go home and tell your wife what you heard in school today? And nothing we were talking about was going to change the test scores, and we both knew that was true.

Then I was standing up and he had his arm around me saying something about how disappointed he was in me because he felt I could do so much better. I guess that meant he thought there was more to me than he was seeing.

I thought there was more to me than he was seeing, too.

I left Mr. Lyons's office feeling bad like I knew I would and thinking he's feeling just like he knew he would. Maybe he was frustrated and wishing something else would happen, but it didn't.

I didn't want to go straight home after school, so I hung out for a while in the school yard until they started closing the gates. Mr. Lyons was okay, but I was mad at him. Nothing that was happening was his fault and it didn't make any sense, but I still felt mad at him because I wanted him to know what was going on in my life and I didn't know how to tell him.

"I CAN USE A HIT," I said. "You holding?"

"You know I'm not holding," Kelly said. "But let me ask you—what you need Lauryn for? All you want to be married to is your habit."

"Ain't you married to your habit? Ain't you married to sitting up here shooting up being spooky? Or you just skimming and saying you don't have a jones?"

Kelly looked over at me, and his stare sent a chill through me. It wasn't mean but like he was looking right into me and didn't like what he saw. It flat out scared me, and I looked away from him. I could feel he had a power over me. All this crap with the television, the questions he was asking me, he was knowing things about me I didn't even know.

"Hey, Kelly, where's all this going?" I asked him. I felt myself holding my breath.

"Yo, Lil J, check it out," Kelly said.

He had turned off the television.

"Why you do that?" I asked. "Turn the sucker back on, man."

"In a minute," Kelly said. "But check this out. You say I'm getting off on being spooky. I can deal with that, Lil J. It ain't everything I would like, man, but it's something I'm being. Can you get next to that? You ain't being that stuff you getting from Dusty or the Girl you scored in Houston. That stuff is being you. It's telling you what to do. It's telling you where to go. It's telling you what to think. How are you dealing with that?"

"Put the television back on."

"Why you need a hit?"

"If you ain't holding, what difference does it make?"

Kelly took the remote and put the television on. It was on a regular station. Some woman was watching her children run around the room. Everywhere they ran some little germs or something was following them. Then she sprayed everything and the germs disappeared.

"Why you watching that?" I asked Kelly.

"What you want to watch?"

I didn't know what he wanted me to say. He had to know that I wanted to know what was on the street. I wanted to see the other stuff he was showing me, too. Stuff about my life and whatnot. I thought he knew more about me than he was saying, that when I talked to him about needing a hit, he would understand.

"What you want to watch?" he asked again. He was flicking through the channels. They were all regular channels.

"Can I tell you why I said I need a hit?"

"They're your minutes," Kelly said.

"When I was a kid, I started carrying around some thoughts," I said. "At first it was like I was carrying them around with me to think about now and again, but then it was a little like I just had them on my mind all the time.

"Maybe I'm wrong, but I think some people walk around and think about germs or something, like the woman in the commercial. I look at her and think she's got germs on her mind and then she'll switch to that spray stuff and then she'll be thinking about her children. When her husband gets home she'll be running her mouth to him, telling him about whatever little thing she was doing all day and he'll tell her what he was doing and they'll be thinking about that. Me, I don't think about nothing else but the things that get me down. It's like the sad part of me is taking over my whole life."

"I got to go to the bathroom," Kelly said.

"Just sit there, sucker!" I lifted the Nine and pointed it dead at him. "I'm trying to tell you something."

Kelly stood up and started past me. "Go on and shoot, Lil J," he said. "You got the power."

He threw the remote in my lap and moved, almost like a shadow, past me and into the hallway.

I wanted to do something, but I didn't know what. I looked at the remote and then at the television. I put the Nine down, knowing I didn't have no power. My thumb moved over the button, but I put that sucker down on the arm of the chair in a hurry. I didn't want to deal with my own life. No way.

I sat there, listening to see if I could hear Kelly. I wondered what he was doing, and then I felt my heart jumping in my chest. I was scared. It was almost like I was getting dope sick again. I was needing some help in a hurry.

"Yo! Kelly!" I called to him. "Kelly!"

I was imagining me on the roof with the gun upside my head. I was imagining me with my eyes closed.

"Yo, Kelly!" I called to him again. "Yo, please come back, man!"

Kelly came back into the room and took the remote from the armrest. When he passed me, his leg went right next to mine, but it didn't touch me, or I didn't feel it. He sat down in his chair and I felt myself breathing easier.

"I'm sorry I got uptight," I said.

"You need some sleep?" Kelly asked.

"I'm not tired," I said.

"You look tired," Kelly said. "You sitting there all droopy looking. Your mouth hanging open."

"You ain't the prettiest sucker in the world either," I said. "What you checking me out so close for anyway? You funny or something?"

"Don't front me," Kelly said.

"I'm sorry."

"Hey, that's different. What you thinking about that cop's family? What you think they doing now?"

"Being sad," I said. "Being miserable. Depending on how it turned out."

"Yeah, there's a lot of sadness in the world, Lil J," Kelly said. "I think that's because when you know your situation, you bring a judgment to it and it don't make a difference if that judgment is right or wrong. You own it either way."

"Or somebody could bring their judgment and lay it on you," I said.

"Yeah, like you were mad at that teacher because he didn't know your situation, and yet you weren't going to let him know what was going down, because it made you feel bad, right?"

"Something like that at first," I said. "Then it come to me that I wasn't really mad at Mr. Lyons—not mad at him personally. What I was mad at was the feeling that I was in a different place, a bad place, and nobody could get next to where I was."

"The silence was creeping in," Kelly said.

"I don't exactly know what you mean about that silence stuff," I said. "But I knew I was mad when I left school that day. I went to the park and hung out. Then, for some stupid reason, I decided to stay in the park all night."

"Spread the stink around so everybody know how you were feeling," Kelly said.

"Something like that, but I didn't put it the way you putting it," I said. "You can talk good. Not pretty, but you got a little weight on you. I bet I can outrhyme you, though. When I spit my rhymes, I sometimes get into a whole 'nother place. I'm like reaching and preaching on a new level. You ever try rapping? Maybe you could DJ if you were carrying enough tunes. What you got going on?"

"I got my place here and I got my television

and I got my remote," Kelly said. "What you got is sleeping in the park all night."

"No, I didn't sleep in the park all night," I said. "Trees and stuff is too scary in the dark. You know, you see the branches moving or the wind, making the leaves rustle like they're whispering something in the dark, and it gets hairy. Plus, you be thinking about all those movies you've seen and you think that maybe one of those serial killers is hanging out in the park looking for his next victim.

"So I went to my apartment building, but I didn't go right home. I went up on the roof to sleep. Just like . . ."

"Just like you ain't got no place to go and you're not in a hurry to move on," Kelly said.

"What you're saying is the same thing everybody else is running down and I can hear it's the word," I said. "But—square business—I'm not out here looking for no garbage cans to curl up in. I'm looking for the same good dreams everybody else is hoping for, but I don't see where they are. Or maybe I see where they are, but I don't see how to get there. I'm sitting up here rapping to some spooky sucker like you and I wouldn't even want to tell nobody about it, but I don't know what else to do. You can run down how weak my game is all you want, but that ain't making it stronger."

"What happened that night you came home from the park?"

"It was about one o'clock in the morning. I knew that because you can look from my roof over to the funeral parlor across the street and they got a big blue clock in the window," I said. "It was about one o'clock or maybe a little after. I was real mad, and I made a decision that from that moment on I wasn't going to care about nothing in the world—I wasn't going to care about my mother, about school, about nothing. It was like I gave up on living right then and there."

"I thought you was thinking on change," Kelly said.

"I would have run to some change if I knew where change was, man," I said. "Can't you dig that?"

"You ain't no dog, brother," Kelly said. "And you ain't no cat. You're a guy, and looking for a way out of your situation is part of the deal."

"Whatever."

"So you spent the night on the roof?"

"No, because it started to rain and so I went on downstairs into my apartment and went to bed," I said. "That don't sound too good, but it was a different me. That was a me that just didn't care anymore. But I know you're too lame to figure that out."

"No, I'm all over it," Kelly said. "If you tell yourself you don't care, then you don't have to do nothing. Right? Get high. Cop a nod. Move on to the next high."

"Yo, Kelly, why you so hard?" I asked. "On one hand you acting like you hip to the whole scene, and then you're sliding back like you didn't hear nothing but some verbs and nouns, man."

"Lil J, listen to what you're saying. You're talking about how hard it is for you to make the right connections and how you see the right places but can't get to them, and I'm sitting up here watching all this foul mess on television and digging on being spooky, and you think that you and me should be hooking up and making something good happen. Yeah, I can dig where you coming from, but I can't make you walk over to where I am and I can't get to you in no easy way. You talking about loving Lauryn and little Brandon—"

"Brian."

"Little Brian, but you can't even get to them even if it only means walking down the block," Kelly said. "Life happens, brother, but ain't nobody promised easy."

He was right. I did want easy. More than that, I thought I was due some damned easy.

The sound of a helicopter surprised me, and I went to the window. It was daylight already, and I asked Kelly what time it was.

"Ten minutes past six," he said.

"What kind of watch you got?"

"Timex."

"Timex? That ain't saying nothing," I said. "You should get you a Rolex. That helicopter is over a Hundred and Twenty-fifth Street. Probably talking about the traffic. I'm thinking about getting up out of here. About seven-thirty, when everybody hits the streets, I'll split."

Kelly started flipping through the channels. He called me over to check out what he was watching. It was that guy on NBC with the long face.

> *Police Officer Anthony Gaffione is stubbornly clinging to life today after being viciously shot by drug dealers in Harlem. Gaffione, the father of two small daughters, was working undercover in an area known for drug activity. Police have made one arrest, nineteen-year-old Rico Brown, and are now searching for the shooter.*

Then my picture came up on the screen and the guy was still talking.

> *Jeremy Dance's street name is Lil J. He is armed and considered extremely dangerous. Police officers all over the city*

and in nearby Jersey City, where Lil J is said to have gang connections, are in a desperate search for the alleged accomplice in the shooting.

I understand we have Mrs. Gaffione on the line. Mrs. Gaffione, we wish you the best of luck in what has to be a difficult time. How are you holding up?

"All we have is our prayers that Tony pulls through. I know he'll never be the same and neither will we."

Mrs. Gaffione, believe me, all of New York will be praying for your brave husband.

"They're gonna kill me, man. I know that. They out looking for me and they getting ready to kill me. Rico told them I was the shooter and there's no way I'm going to stand there and shoot nobody for nothing. All that's on Rico and his dope. Now my life is over. That's it, my life is over."

"What you crying for if you don't care?" Kelly asked.

"What you mean what I'm crying for?" I asked. "Would you want your life to be over on some jive humble like this? They ain't going to believe me. They're going to believe Rico because he got his story all in the papers and on television. They're going to put his ass in jail for fifty-leven years and they're going to put me in jail for that much and two dimes more! What that punk Rico is thinking about is, if that cop dies they're going to be talking about the death penalty—like they got on that dude from Staten Island. He's going to keep on lying on me to save hisself."

"So what you going to do?"

"Nothing to do. I can't stay here and I can't go out there because they're going to kill me," I said. "That's what they really want to do. They don't want no trial. They want some chalk around my body."

"So what you going to do?" Kelly asked again. "You're saying you can't stay here and—"

"Yo, Kelly, shut the hell up!"

Silence. Only the distant sound of the helicopter and the close-up sound of me sniffling. It was like my whole life was falling apart in one long, horrible moment. All those times of not knowing what to do and feeling bad were being rolled into one straight-out nightmare.

"Yo, Kelly, you think this is how hell is?"

"How I know?"

"Fast-forward that picture again," I said.

Kelly clicked the remote and I saw the street below. There were cops everywhere. Some were dressed in SWAT gear.

"Not the street," I said. "Show me on the roof landing."

"That's where you want to be?" Kelly asked. "You ready to throw it all away?"

I didn't say nothing, just looked at the screen. After a while Kelly had the picture. I was sliding along the wall as I was going up the staircase. I looked hurt. Maybe it was my arm hurting, or maybe I had been shot again. I couldn't tell. Then there was me sitting on the roof landing. My face was twisted and my eyes looked so dark. My hand was trembling as I lifted the Nine.

"Stop! Stop it!"

"THIS IS GETTING TOO HARD for me," I said. "You okay, man, but looking at myself on television—checking out my life—is hard. I don't see nothing that good about it."

"I saw a guy on *Cops* one time," Kelly said. "He was half drunk and walking up to the police calling out, 'Shoot me! Shoot me!' and pointing to his chest."

"He was ready to give up the struggle," I said.

"I didn't think he really wanted to die. He just wanted to keep telling himself that it didn't make a difference so he didn't have to do nothing about his life," Kelly said.

"Who you to be judging people?" I asked. "They don't show your picture on no magazine covers."

"I'm hip. You need a soda or something?"

"You got some sodas up in here?"

"In the drawers under that closet," Kelly said.

Sometimes Kelly seemed okay, but I didn't trust him completely. Why didn't he tell me about the sodas before? I almost didn't even go for it, but then I wanted a soda bad.

The closet was built in and the drawers were on the bottom. I opened the closet doors first and looked in. Nothing. The right-hand drawer was tight, and it hurt my arm trying to get it open. But there, like Kelly had said, was a cardboard container with six bottles of soda.

"You want one too?" I asked.

"Yeah, okay."

I took out two sodas. They weren't cold, but I was still looking forward to something to drink.

"Where's the opener?"

"I don't have one," Kelly said. "You can open them in the bathroom. There's a nail on the back of the door."

"You ain't even got an opener," I said. "That's weak."

"I manage," Kelly said. "And you don't have to drink the soda if you don't want it."

I went back down the hallway toward the bathroom. There was a noise and I froze. I could hear something scurrying across the floor. Rats. I held my breath for a moment and then went into the bathroom. There was a nail in the back of the door. I thought about somebody coming in to take a bath and hanging their robe on the door. With the smell and the rats, the building had probably been empty for at least a year. I wondered how long Kelly had been up in there. As far as I was concerned, he could have been crazy. On the other hand maybe it was just his get-over. A lot of homeless dudes were living in abandoned buildings. Most of them had strung some wires up to telephone poles for electricity. That's what Kelly had probably done.

I messed around in the dark until I got the bottle top against the nail and pulled it down to open the bottle. Then I did the other one and took them both out to Kelly.

He was watching the street below. It was morning, and down the street there was a television truck with its high antenna.

"After a while something else is going to happen and all this is going to quiet down," I told Kelly. "Then they won't even remember who I am."

"Who are you?"

"You know who I am."

"I know your name," Kelly said. "But who do you see when you look in the mirror?"

The soda was piss warm, but it was good. I didn't realize how hungry I was. "Hey, Kelly, you got any bacon and eggs?" I asked.

"So who you see when you look in the mirror?" he asked again.

"Who I see?" Kelly was drinking from his bottle, and I could see the light from the television along the glass as he lifted it. I turned and saw the shades, and they were light. "Sometimes I don't see nobody," I said. "You know, you got to be something first, and then you see what you're being. Like, say a roach crawl across a mirror.

He don't know he's a roach. I don't even know if a roach can see.

"When I was a kid I used to look at myself in the mirror all the time and pretend I was a superhero. Sometimes I would be G.I. Joe, and sometimes I would be Batman. Then one time I had a bad day—I was still a kid—and after that I had trouble seeing myself."

"What happened?"

"I don't know."

"You don't know or you don't want to deal with it?" Kelly asked.

"Same difference, ain't it?"

Kelly clicked the remote. I saw a playing field, and then there was P.S. 125 on 123rd Street. The class was sitting at their desks, and when I saw Anita Vega, I knew I had to be somewhere in the class.

"You getting excited, Lil J?" Kelly asked.

"Yeah, man, you got the thing back on the day. I was kind of cool then. I remember my mother was talking to my father the night before. She told him it was going to be my birthday, and he said he would come by after school and pick me up and take me out for some pizza. I was real excited about that.

"That teacher, that's Miss Petridis. She had the best third-grade class in the school. Every day she spent fifteen minutes talking about something in American history, and each of us had to write down two things that were special about the day.

"We were studying about the Revolutionary War and how brave all the American soldiers were. If you raised your hand in class when Miss Petridis asked questions, she would give you a gold star on a card at the end of the day. The card would have your name on it and the date. I was thinking that I would raise my hand a lot and get a gold star to show my father when he picked me up.

"Miss Petridis had a DVD about the war. She even let us boo the bad guys. You know, those were the redcoats.

"'It's like the Red Sox,'" she said. 'Every true Yankees fan hates the Red Sox, and back in the days of the Revolutionary War the Americans who were fighting for their freedom were called Yankees.'

"You can see how she had everybody in the class all excited. I could almost feel like I was standing up in the boat with George Washington waiting to cross the Delaware. I wanted that gold star real bad, but I thought I had messed up when I had one more question even though she said we was going on to silent reading. What I asked her was were there any Americans still around, and she gave me this funny look.

" 'Class, can we tell Jeremy where the Americans are today?' she asked.

"As usual, Sarah's hand went up. 'They're still at Valley Forge,' she said.

"Miss Petridis laughed and explained how we were all Americans. That made me feel proud and everything, but none of the pictures she showed looked like me or any of my friends.

"There's me on the corner waiting for my father. I didn't know he was going to bring Eddie. Eddie is his other son. He's a little younger than me and he used to be skinny, but now he's kind of cut. When he showed up with Eddie, I was disappointed. Eddie had something with him in a box and he brought it to the pizza place."

An image of me and Eddie sitting at the table in the pizza place. My father was talking on his cell phone and Eddie and I were eating pizza. The pizza was okay, but it wasn't nothing special, because Eddie was there and he lived with my father. All the time we was eating, I thought that maybe Eddie had a present for me in the box he was carrying. When me and him finished our slices, my father told him to show me what he had in the box. It was a trophy he had won playing basketball in the Biddy League.

My father didn't say nothing about my birthday, and I figured he had just forgot about it.

"Then he took me home in his car. He dropped me off right in front of the house. When I went upstairs, I was kind of down. I still had my card with the gold star in my pocket, and when I felt it, I took it out and looked at it. Then I looked in the mirror to see if I could look like an American. When I was looking at me, I didn't think I looked like an American or nothing else. That's why I say you got to figure out what you about first and *then* look in the mirror. You know what I mean?"

"You have any trouble opening the soda?" Kelly asked.

"Why you going there?" I asked. "What you care if I had trouble opening the soda? You drinking, ain't you?"

"You got any money?" Kelly asked. "I could go out and see if I can get us something to eat."

"I ain't hungry."

"Yeah, you hungry," Kelly came back. "You just more scared than you hungry. You scared if I go out I might turn you in. You scared if I go out I might not come back. You scared to be alone with that gun. You scared of the remote. You scared to look in the mirror. Lil J, what you ain't scared of?"

"So you the big-deal encyclopedia brother," I said. "You need to be walking around with a cape and an outfit with a big EB on it so everybody know you got all the answers. Yo, Kelly, you got ears, bro, but you don't hear all that tough," I said. "Everything that's me ain't all my fault."

"That's the deal," Kelly said. "You got to find a way to make your life all your fault."

"No, man, what I got to do is to get through today," I said. "And if you don't know what that's about, then you probably ain't black enough, or ain't poor enough, or ain't been beat down enough to get next to it."

I COULD FEEL MYSELF GETTING mad, wanting to go upside Kelly's head. And I could hear myself thinking that my mad wasn't working with him. It didn't make no difference to him, but it was making a difference to me. He had been talking to me all night and listening to me and showing me things about myself that I didn't even know. Now it was morning and we was sitting being quiet with me out there on the edge like I always was and him sitting in that chair looking away from me, his shoulders kind of slumped forward, looking smaller than he should have been.

"Yo, Kelly, I ain't really trying to play hard,

man," I said. "But I thought you were digging where I'm coming from."

"You want me to dig it or you expecting me to bust out with some applause?" Kelly asked.

"Just understand, man."

Silence. I thought I could hear his breathing, but I wasn't sure. From somewhere I could smell bacon cooking. A picture came into my mind of some woman making breakfast for her boy. I was thinking the boy was happy.

"Can you get my mother on the television?"

"Probably won't come in clear," he said. "You ain't really thinking about her, are you?"

"Yeah, I am," I said. "But let's check the news first."

Kelly clicked the remote and there was a man, a woman, and a little girl standing in front of some microphones. The sound was down low, and I asked Kelly to make it a little louder.

> *My husband is holding on. He's always been a fighter. He took my hand and whispered that he loved me.*

I watched as the woman started crying and the man next to her put his arm around her. The little girl leaned against the woman and put her face against her side. A caption appeared under the picture:

MRS. SHERRI GAFFIONE, WIFE OF WOUNDED OFFICER ANTHONY GAFFIONE, GIVES STATEMENT ON CONDITION OF HUSBAND.

It made me feel terrible to see her crying and I started crying, too. It was just so hard to figure that I was part of this whole scene, and yet, there it was. It was me. Like Kelly said, it had to be somebody's fault, and if it was about my life, then I had to make it my fault.

The news switched to a tornado in Tennessee and Kelly clicked the remote again. The picture came in black and white with only a touch of color, like it needed adjustment. There was somebody laying on a bed, face to the wall. On the little night table there were some pill bottles. Mama. I couldn't tell what pills they were. I knew I had taken some of her pain pills. She wasn't moving.

"She okay?"

"What you mean by 'okay'?" Kelly asked.

"I mean . . . you know . . . she ain't moving," I said.

Kelly didn't say nothing. We watched my mother for a while. For most of the time she was still, but then she moved her arm and wiped at her face. At least she was alive. I put my head down in my hands. I didn't want to see her anymore.

"You need a hit?" Kelly asked. "I could go out and find something in this neighborhood."

"Fuck off."

"Don't you want to stop feeling bad?" Kelly went on. "Ain't you dope sick? Don't your nerves feel all jagged and messed around? Don't you want to get away?"

"Away from this place? This raggedy apartment?"

"No, I mean, away from you," Kelly said. "Isn't that what you're running from?"

"You were talking about me changing something before," I said. "Me changing one thing in my life. What happened to all that talk?"

"You are changing things," Kelly said. "You changing that woman's life. You changing that cop's life. You changing your mama's life. Don't you want a hit so you can nod on out of here?"

"No, I don't," I said.

"That's good," Kelly said.

"Yeah, but it's a lie. You probably know it's a lie too. I want a hit so bad, I feel like my head is screaming for it. Nothing sounds better than being away from this mess. Nothing sounds better right now than getting higher than the hole I'm in. I know you can't imagine it, but I can almost feel it. Even when I'm getting nervous, cooking up the hit, I start to feel better. And when I do the hit, and my face is all flushed and the tingling in my fingers has started and then there's nothingness like I didn't even weigh but an ounce and the world is floating, drifting away from me. Then I feel human.

"Kelly, you can't tell me nothing about getting high, man," I said. "I know every hit is steady downhill and all the things that can happen when I'm using. But with that stuff in me I can shut out the voices that say *Wrong* and *You ain't nothing* and *You ain't going nowhere*. When I'm straight, I can't keep them voices out my head. But when I'm high, I don't hear no voices. Nothing putting me down.

"You talking about what I see when I look in the mirror, and I'm telling you I don't see nothing, but you don't know how that feels. You can't get there; right?"

"You want another soda?" Kelly came back.

"What I really want is to be away from here," I said. "Away from your warm soda, away from this stink hole you living in, and away from all you running your mouth. You can talk 'til you turn blue and it don't make no difference 'cause the real deal ain't different. Look at me, man. I don't need no true. I need some *different*."

"Yeah, could be. But everything you reaching for ain't really different. You know what you said just now?" Kelly turned and looked at me. "About how when you get high, you get all flushed and you feel so light and the world is floating away?"

"Yeah, I know what I said, and I know what I feel," I said.

"Good, because that's just the way dying feels, too," Kelly said. "And when you get to that point—when you know you dying—you're going to feel just as sick and disgusted with yourself and you'll be wishing just as hard that you made something of your life, that you created something. Maybe something small, like a relationship with you and Lauryn and Brian. Maybe something even smaller, a way to get to know yourself enough not to mind looking in a mirror."

"You don't know what dying is about, Kelly," I said. "You ain't that damn smart."

"Don't bet on it, Lil J," he said. "Don't bet on it."

"It don't bother me that much if I'm not thinking about it," I said. "Maybe I'm getting used to it."

"Yeah, that's funny, huh?" Kelly clicked to Oprah's show. "Something hurts you real bad and you get used to it. Like being hurt becomes part of who you are."

"Sometimes I sit and watch television when things go wrong," I said. "Or I play video games. You know, take my mind someplace else. Remember that white girl I told you about? Sabrina? She used to say that for her television was like methadone. You couldn't really get high, but you could, like, walk away from the stuff that's messing with your mind."

"So you chilling out with Oprah?" Kelly asked.

"I didn't ask you to put Oprah on," I said. "You turned her on. Why don't you get back to the street?"

Kelly pointed the remote at the screen, then stopped and threw it to me. I went for it with both hands and got a sharp pain in my left arm. The remote fell and rattled across the wooden floor. I realized I had been holding my arm against my side the whole time. When I tried to move it, even a little, it hurt like hell.

"You got anything for pain?" I asked Kelly.

"No." A little sharp answer, like he was mad or something.

I picked up the remote. There were numbers on the bottom half, from zero to nine, and I thought they must have been for the different channels. Above that there were four colored buttons, red, green, yellow, and blue. The red button had two arrows pointing to the left. The green had one arrow pointing to the left, the yellow had an arrow pointing to the right, and the blue had two arrows pointing to the right. On the very bottom there was a button with a black square in the middle of it.

"Which buttons should I push?" I asked Kelly.

"Try them," he said.

I thought about him showing the picture of me on the roof landing. One time I had had the Nine up to my head and my eyes squeezed shut. I didn't want to go back to that. If the buttons with the two arrows made things go fast-forward or fast-backward, I wouldn't know what to do if I came on that scene again.

"What happens if I mess up?" I asked Kelly. "Get on something I don't want?"

"Isn't that the way things go?" he asked. "Sometimes you do all right and sometimes . . . sometimes you don't."

I stood up and started toward Kelly to give him back the remote, but got this real cold feeling. It was like there was something between me and him that kept me at a distance.

"Why don't you take the remote?" I asked. "You know how to use it."

"I'm not the one that needs to be changing, Lil J," Kelly said. "You've been talking about how you need to get in some better place, and how your dope is getting you so you don't feel the weight anymore. You're tired of being blown around by whatever stink wind that comes along. You don't need to be lighter and you don't need to deal with the wind. You need to be the wind. Take the remote."

"No, I can't," I said. "I'm too scared, Kelly. No lie. I can't do it, man. I'm sorry. I'm so sorry."

Kelly put the remote down on the arm of his chair.

"I think you are sorry," he said.

"You mad?" I asked.

"Just tired," Kelly said. "I been up awhile."

He clicked the remote and I could see the street again. The television news trucks weren't there anymore, but there were a lot more cops. We watched for a few minutes, and I thought about asking Kelly to switch to a news station, but I didn't.

I was tired and my arm was hurting bad again.

This time it was like a throbbing pain. I looked at my hand and it was swollen pretty bad. It didn't make no difference if I could get out of the building, because I needed to get to some kind of hospital.

"Kelly, I need to get this over with," I said. "Can you call the police with your cell? Tell them I'm up here and I want to give up?"

"You do it," he said. He laid the cell phone on the floor and gave it a push with his foot.

"You know I'm not that bad a guy," I said. "What you think? You think I'm going to be in jail for the rest of my life?"

"How I know?"

"You can look at it on your television," I said. "That's how you know. The same as you been doing all night long!"

"No, Lil J, what's going to happen to you depends on what you going to do, not what's on the television," Kelly said. "And right now what you doing is sitting there waiting to see what everybody else is going to do. The cell phone is there if you want to call the police. Pick it up. Or if you think you bad enough, grab your Nine and shoot your way out."

I couldn't see myself in jail for the rest of my life. And if Rico got over with his story, I might even get the death penalty. And I knew in my heart that I didn't want to shoot anybody or get shot up myself. Everything that happened started going through my head, and it was just as clear as it was on television. I thought about me and Rico at Dusty's place, tapping the bags of dope, going to meet the guy who turned out to be a cop, and the shooting.

We had gone back to Rico's and I remembered being so shook up I couldn't think straight. Rico was talking some crap about how the cop thought he was slick and I kept asking him if he had shot him or just scared him.

"Yeah, I capped the sucker!" he had said.

I went into the bathroom and threw up. What I wanted to do was to beat Rico to a bloody pulp. But then I remembered the guns were still on the table and . . . *Shit!*

"Kelly, suppose Rico switched guns?" I said.

"SUPPOSE THE GUN I GOT was the one he shot the cop with? Maybe that's why he's saying I'm the shooter!" I said.

"So what you saying?" Kelly stood up.

I was surprised to see him stand and face me. He seemed even taller than he had before, as if he had changed and had grown so that he was more than I was. When we had first met, I had just taken him for some homeless dude with maybe some street smarts. Now he was standing, looking at me, and I thought I was feeling something coming out of him, but something in him that I could sense, that I was sure was there. A power.

He looked at me, waiting for me to say something. "I want to take back that minute," I said, "when I was being sick in the bathroom."

"Yeah, okay," he said reaching for the remote, "but suppose he didn't switch Nines. Maybe the police don't know what gun was used to shoot the cop?"

"So why he saying . . . ?" I didn't know what to do. Kelly sat down and shook his head like he was getting tired of me. "It don't matter what gun I got. I have to get rid of it before the police get here."

"You still want me to call them?"Kelly asked.

"No."

"Yo, Lil J." Kelly put one leg over the side of the chair, the way I do sometimes. "You thinking the world is supposed to stand still while you make up your mind how you want to live? You thinking everybody supposed to freeze in place while you bopping around doing your thing?"

"I ain't *bopping around*," I said.

"You came here huffing and puffing with a gun

in your hand," Kelly said. "That was last night and this is morning and you still standing there huffing and puffing with the gun in your hand. You going to shoot your way out or not?"

"I just need some time to think, man."

"You don't even know what time is," Kelly said.

"You the one holed up in here and ain't got no life," I said. "I'm stone street. I know what's going down. And I didn't learn it from no television, either."

"You know what's going down?" Kelly asked. "No, I don't think so." He picked up the remote and clicked it twice. There was the picture of me on the roof again with the gun up to my head.

"Kelly, stop it!" I said. I turned my head away from the screen. "Come on, man!"

From the corner of my eye I could see that the screen had gone dark. I looked at it slow and saw that the television was on another channel. I was looking at an advertisement for a household cleanser. My legs were weak as I found my chair and sat down.

"Hey, Lil J, what you thinking that picture was?" Kelly asked in this real quiet voice. "You thinking that was the future? Something down the road and you looking to see which road it's on so you can change direction? Your mind just running loose, going every which way? Like you were thinking that maybe Rico switched the guns?

"Or you thinking that maybe that picture is just another 'right now' trailing after you, looking to catch up with you while you standing still trying to make up your mind? What you thinking, Lil J?"

"I'll leave the gun here," I said. "And I'll go outside and give myself up."

"I don't want the gun up in here," Kelly said. "I didn't have a gun when you got here and I don't need one now."

"If the cops see me coming out with a gun in my hand . . ." I knew that's all they needed and they would blow me away. "Kelly, give me some kind of break, okay? Look, you young and everything, but you got some smarts. I know this whole thing is my messed-up bag, not yours. But I really need some help.

"You keep asking me what I want to take back, and the deeper I go, the more I see I can't get no place comfortable, you know what I mean? I'm looking to find the place where my thing went wrong. Right now it look to me like, with Rico out there flapping his lips on me, that I'm gone, just gone. You shoot a cop in New York and nobody wants to hear nothing. They need to burn somebody, and they ain't going to be caring too much who it is they burning. I ain't got a chance and I don't think I've ever had a chance. And what little piece of hope I got, you know, for a miracle or something, is gone if they catch me with the Nine. This is your turf, brother. Can you get rid of the gun for me? Please?"

Kelly looked me up and down, then stood and came over to me. We were standing close for the first time, with him no more than a few inches away from me. I was spooked. It was like he was looking at me and through me at the same time. He put out his hand and I handed him the gun.

Kelly turned and walked slowly over to the window. He stood for a while, and I thought I saw his shoulders heave as if he was taking a deep breath. I was thinking maybe he was relieved that I wasn't holding the gun.

He pulled the string on the shade and let it go flapping up to the top of the window. I blinked as daylight flooded the room. I saw Kelly open the window, and felt the cool air against my skin.

Blam! Blam!

He was shooting down into the street!

"WHAT YOU DOING? WHAT YOU doing?" I heard myself screaming. I took a step toward the window and stopped. My head was going crazy. I didn't know what to do.

Blam! Blam!

He shot again.

Kelly turned and went back to the chair. He picked up the remote and turned the television set on. It was the street. The cops were pointing up. I knew they had to be pointing toward the window. I could feel my heart pounding in my chest.

On the screen the cops were ducking behind

their cars. A close-up shot had one of them putting on his bulletproof vest.

"Kelly!" I crouched down near the chair. "Use the remote, man. Use the remote! Take me back to when I was with Rico! Take the whole day back. Can you do that?"

"That's not going to make your life better," Kelly said. He was standing with his head sideways, looking at the screen. "You said that already."

"I don't know that, Kelly. Maybe it will. Maybe . . . I don't know . . . " I was half talking and half crying. "I don't know that—why you shoot out the window? Why you shoot . . . ? Kelly, if you can take something back— Oh, man! Oh, man!

"Kelly, check out the screen, they coming into the building! They coming in!"

On the screen I could see the SWAT guys, all dressed in black, running in a line, their automatic weapons pointing up. They didn't look like people—they looked like some kind of crazy animals with guns for arms. I felt like I was in a storm. My whole life was spinning around me. I was jerking my head from the screen toward the window.

From out in the street came the sounds of sirens and people shouting. There was a bang, and then I smelled smoke.

"Kelly! Please! What we going to do?" My voice was cracking, and I could hear myself start to stutter. Then I saw Kelly headed toward the door. He still had the gun in his hand. "Kelly, where you going? Where you going?"

"Get some rest, Lil J," he said. "I got to go."

"Yo, man, don't leave me now. Please."

Kelly went out the door. I took a half step toward it and stopped. I wanted to run, but I was too scared. My legs weren't working. I looked at the television. I saw the SWAT team was coming up the stairs, one flight at a time.

I got down in the middle of the floor and spread my arms out so they would see I didn't have no gun. I closed my eyes as tight as I could and tried not to move.

Then I heard shots! I wanted to get up and go to the stairs and scream down that I'd give up, but I was too scared to move.

"I give up! I give up!" I called out from the floor. "Oh, God, I give up!"

There were more shots, and then nothing.

A few seconds passed and then a few minutes. I heard sirens and the squealing of tires. The sound of a helicopter drew near and then faded away. I kept my head down, waiting.

The television was still on, and I looked up at it. It was the street again. I saw the front of the building, and the SWAT team was coming out. Some of them had their helmets off. The camera switched to an ambulance. The camera must have been jerking as they took an overhead shot of somebody being put into the ambulance. I couldn't see who it was from the floor, and I was too scared to stand up.

I lay on the floor all day. The street noises changed to just passing traffic. At times my whole body shook, and other times it was still and I could hear my pulse pounding in my temples. When I could get up the courage, I lifted my head a little and looked at the screen, but I couldn't really see anything too clear from where I was laying. The wind picked up and made the shades flap and I felt a few drops of rain on the back of my neck.

I didn't know what happened, what the shooting was about, who was being put into the ambulance. I thought about Kelly. Did they shoot him by mistake? Was he just crazy? I didn't know what was going on. I thought I heard noises on the staircase. I thought I heard the wind rattling the windowpanes. I wasn't sure what was real and what was in my mind. When I heard the sound of crying, of someone whimpering and alone in the room, I knew who it was. It was me.

Night came, and the room grew dark except for the light from the television. Then the television went off and I was alone in the blackness of the room. Had someone turned off the electricity? Were they waiting for me to come out, to show them that I was still alive?

Get some rest, Lil J, Kelly had said. *I got to go.*

There was no resting. Every nerve in my body was tense. Every muscle was aching. Getting up off the floor was hard. My body felt weak and my hands were shaking again. My left arm was a little numb, but it didn't seem too bad. My right knee was aching, and I thought I must have hurt it when I was getting down on the floor.

I didn't know what to do. Still. I didn't know.

I pushed the door open. Darkness. The place stunk. It smelled musty, and it was hard to breathe as I eased down the stairs, feeling my way along the walls.

I heard something scurry on the steps below me. Another rat. Me and the rat making our way down the stairs. Me more scared than the rat.

The first floor. The front door was half off its hinges. There was something across the door. At first I couldn't see what it was, and then, when a car swept by, I saw it was yellow police tape. I crawled to the door and looked out. The street was mostly empty. Two men were sitting on a stoop down the block. I didn't see any police cars.

I was on the street, walking slow, trying not to run. I saw myself reflected in the window of a bodega, and I was covered with dust. I brushed myself off as I walked. When I got to my 'hood, I stopped on a corner and looked around for the police. Nothing. I circled the block, looking for strange vans, white guys sitting in cars, anything that might be a trap. I didn't see anything.

Lenox Avenue was busy even though it was late. A woman was selling sausage sandwiches on the street. Two men had rigged up a television by hooking the plug into the base of a streetlamp. They were watching the news. As I stood and watched it, I realized I was cold. I was going to move on when I saw the front of the building I had been in.

After a tense standoff that lasted for hours, and a shootout in which a number of shots were fired at the police, a SWAT team took down a teenager identified by neighborhood street people only as Kelly, the second man in the shooting of undercover police officer Anthony Gaffione. It is not known whether Kelly is the suspect's real name or only his street tag.

The young man came out of the building brandishing what police believed to be a gun but which actually turned out to be a television remote control. Police believe that he chose to be killed by police rather than face a lengthy prison term.

Gaffione, who is expected to fully recover from his injuries, was apprised of the capture as he was being released from the hospital today and has identified the teenager as the second man in the drug bust gone wrong.

The PBA credits the capture to good police work and the determination not to ever let potential cop killers loose on the streets.

Then the television image switched to the one I had seen before, of someone being put into the back of an ambulance. My mouth was dry. I was confused and tired as I stumbled toward my house.

I knew that Kelly was way too smart to just run out in the street pointing a remote at a SWAT team. He was way too cool to just throw away his life. Kelly was special, something else. I knew it and he knew it.

I realized that when he came out the building, he must have been thinking about me, about what would come into my head as I tried to figure it all out. The fear was still in me and pushing against the insides of my skin so hard, I imagined I wouldn't look like me anymore. I would look like something different—not even somebody different. Something different.

I was also thinking that I would see Kelly again. One day he would just show up and look at me the way he did and ask me what was going on in my life. I didn't know what was going on now, but I knew Kelly wouldn't want to hear that shit. He just wouldn't.

"Lil J, you been cleaning sewers in them

clothes?" Thelma Mosley was sitting on the stoop, drinking beer.

"No," I said. "Just doing some work."

I went upstairs, and Mama was in the kitchen, sleeping with her head on the table. There were pills on the table, and I went over to her to see if she was all right. She was breathing shallow, but she looked okay.

"Mama." I shook her shoulder. "Why don't you get up and go to bed?"

She mumbled something about "In a minute."

I went to my bedroom and took off my dirty clothes. I didn't want to be in my underwear in case the cops came, so I put on some clean pants and a fresh shirt before I lay across the bed.

The night played out in my mind over and over again. Sometimes I thought it had happened one way, and then I couldn't be sure. I remembered Kelly asking me if the image of me on the landing, ready to kill myself, was the future I was headed toward or the past creeping up on me as I stayed in one place.

I was afraid of the future, as I had always been. Now I was afraid to stay still, afraid of what was coming after me.

I wanted to sleep, but I wasn't sure enough of what had went down to close my eyes. I got up and walked into the living room. Then I was asking myself if anything that I thought had happened had been real. I had heard about dudes using drugs and getting their brains messed up. Was my brain messed up? I remembered, or thought I remembered, tapping the Baggies with Rico and putting two bags in my pocket. I went back to my bedroom and went through the pockets of my dirty clothes. The Baggies were still there. Or they might have been there from the day before. I took them into the bathroom and dropped them into the toilet, flushed it, and watched as they swirled around in the water and finally disappeared.

I stood in the bathroom awhile, trying to pull myself together. Then I thought about my arm. I took my shirt off again and looked at it. It was sore and swollen. I folded some toilet tissue into a square and poured peroxide on it and wiped the dried blood from around the wound. The library was open over the weekend, and I thought about going there and looking up something on the internet about treating wounds.

I went back to the living room, sat down on the couch, and turned on the television. I looked for the news again. The first two channels just had commercials.

On the next channel there it was, the image of me, sitting on the landing to the roof. This was Kelly talking to me. I knew that the same way I knew I would see him again one day. On the screen I wasn't moving, just sitting there, my eyes closed, my face twisted, like something real bad was going to happen to me. Or maybe was going to catch up with me. I didn't know which. I reached for the remote.